the MUTTS ™

spring diaries

Other Books by Patrick McDonnell

Mutts
Cats and Dogs: Mutts II
More Shtuff: Mutts III
Yesh!: Mutts IV
Our Mutts: Five
A Little Look-See: Mutts VI
What Now: Mutts VII
I Want to Be the Kitty: Mutts VIII
Dog-Eared: Mutts IX
Who Let the Cat Out: Mutts X
Everyday Mutts
Animal Friendly
Call of the Wild
Stop and Smell the Roses
Earl & Mooch
Our Little Kat King
Bonk!
Cat Crazy
Living the Dream
The Mutts Diaries
Playtime
The Mutts Winter Diaries
Year of Yesh
The Mutts Autumn Diaries
#LoveMUTTS

Mutts Sundays
Sunday Mornings
Sunday Afternoons
Sunday Evenings
Best of Mutts

Shelter Stories
A Shtinky Little Christmas

the MUTTS
spring diaries

• PATRICK McDONNELL •

Andrews McMeel
PUBLISHING®

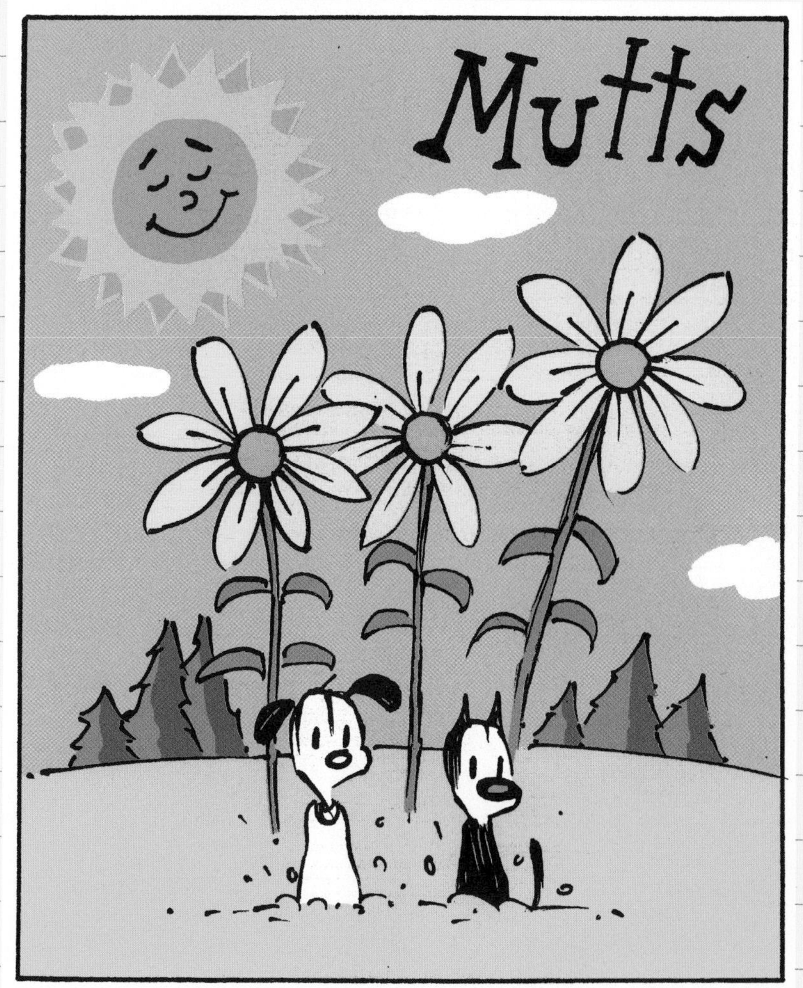
Mutts

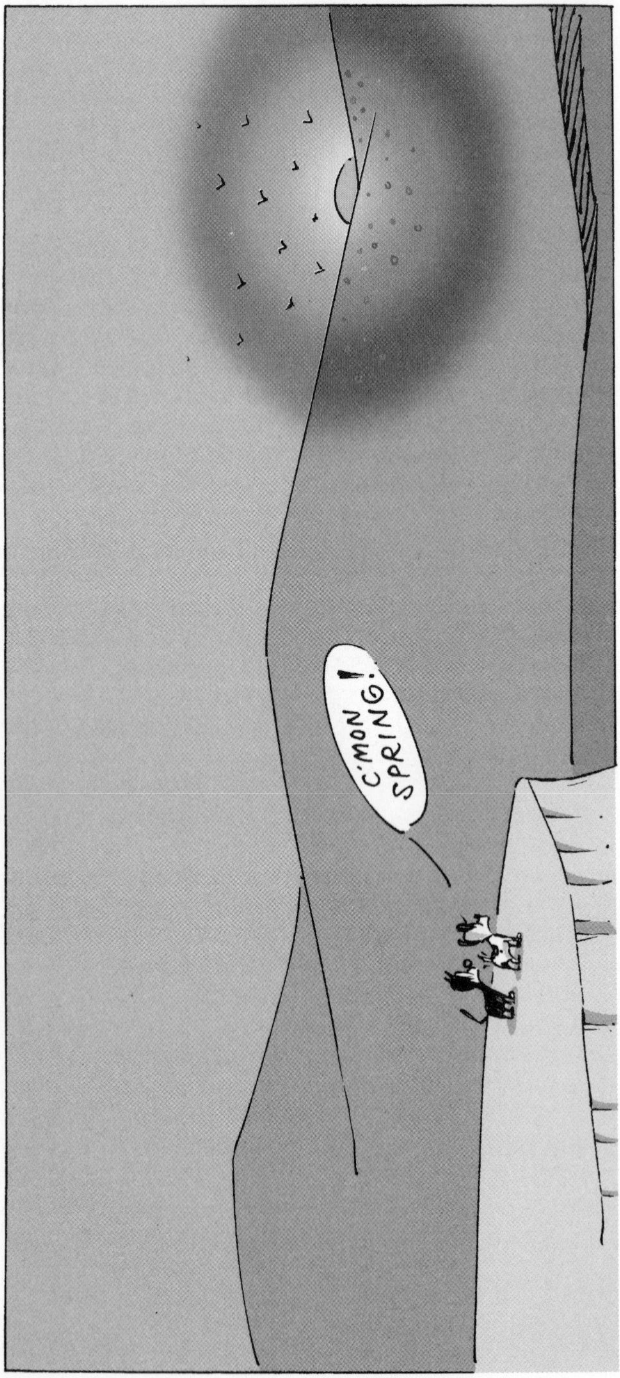
C'MON SPRING!

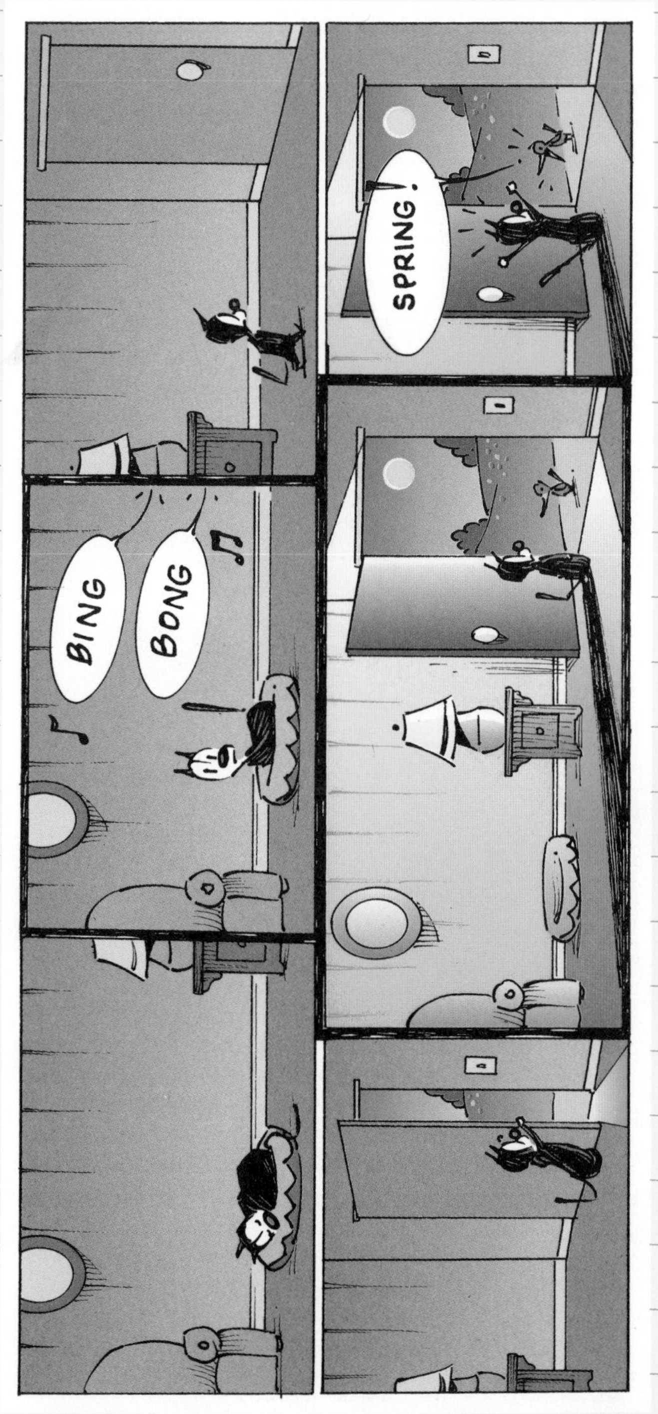
BING
BONG
SPRING!

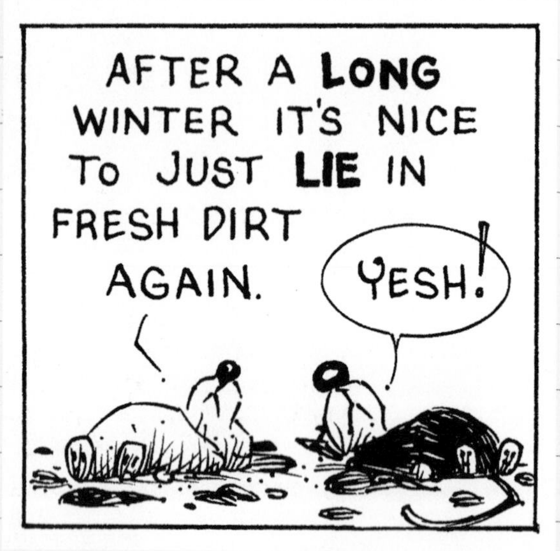
AFTER A LONG WINTER IT'S NICE TO JUST LIE IN FRESH DIRT AGAIN.
YESH!

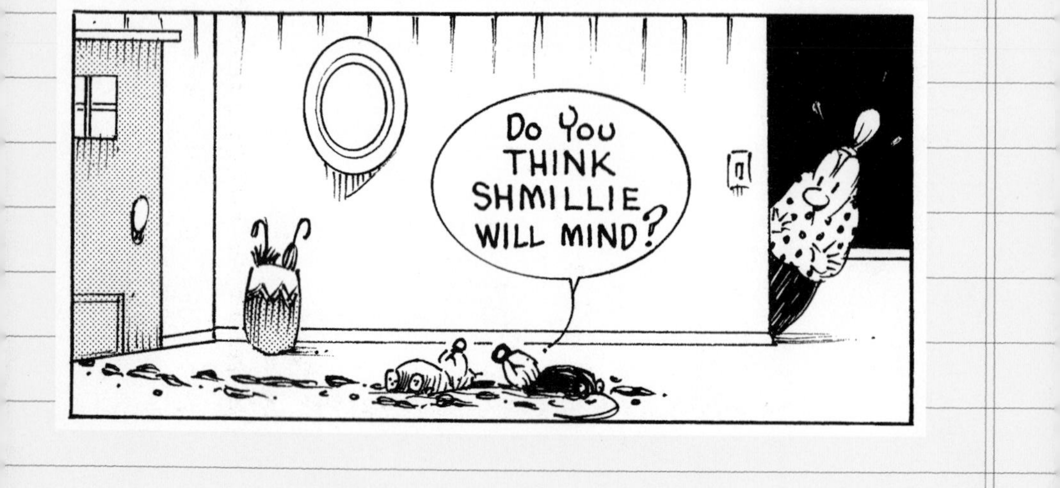
Do You THINK SHMILLIE WILL MIND?

HEY, EARL—WHAT ARE YOU LOOKING FOR?
BIRDS—BUT I DON'T SEE ANY.
THEY ALL SHOULD BE RETURNING FROM THE SOUTH SOON...
SHMAYBE THEY CHARTERED A BUS.

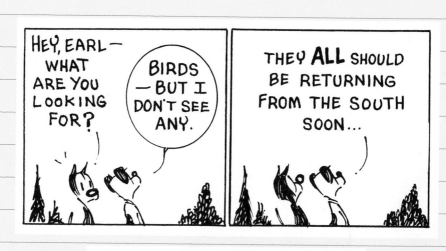

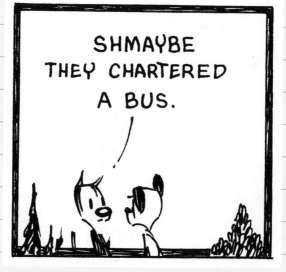

OH, THANK GOODNESS-
WE'RE FINALLY HERE!
FOO
"FOO" IS RIGHT!
WHO EVER HEARD OF A BIRD GETTING AIRSICK.
FOO

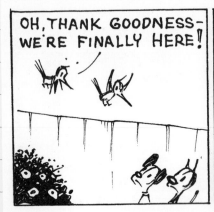

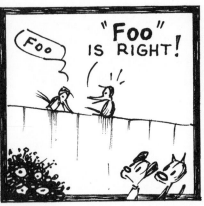

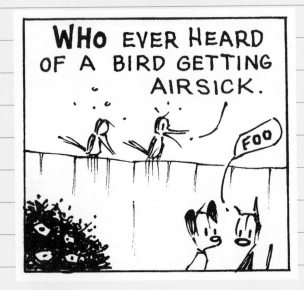

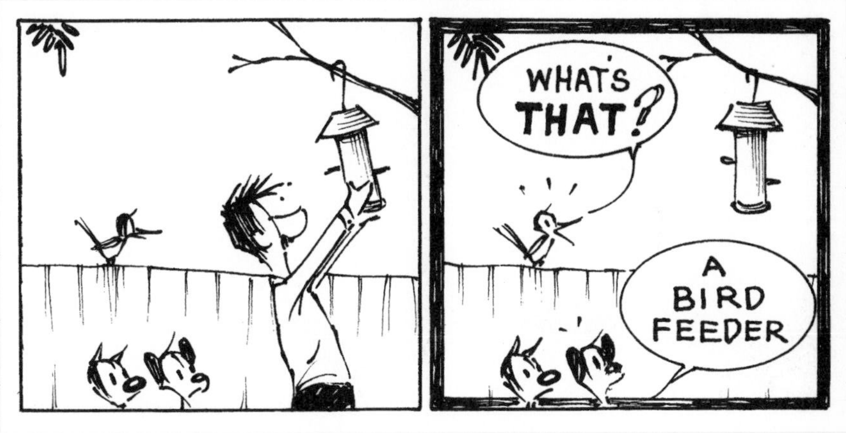
WHAT'S THAT?
A BIRD FEEDER

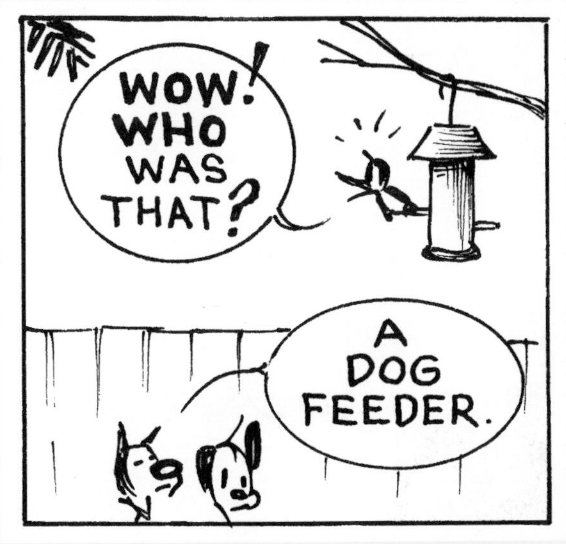
WOW! WHO WAS THAT?
A DOG FEEDER.

MOM...
YES?
CAN I GO OUT AND PLAY?

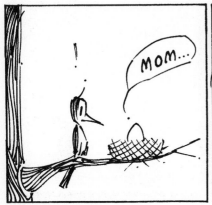

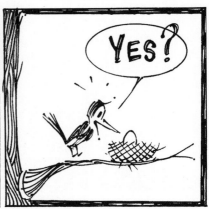

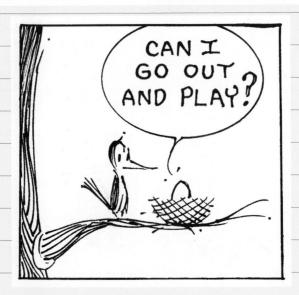

I'M A
SNAPPING
TURTLE.
COOL.
I DIDN'T EVEN
KNOW TURTLES
HAD FINGERS!

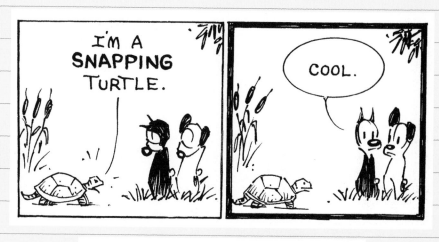

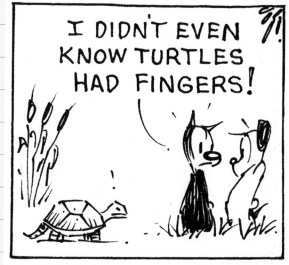

I CARRY MY HOME ON MY BACK.
HMMMM.
I'D JUST CARRY THE KITCHEN.

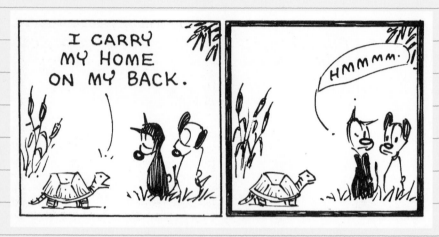

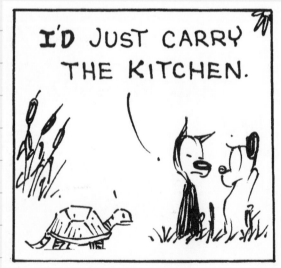

♫ LITTLE PINK ♫ SOCK LITTLE PINK SOCK
OH, LITTLE PINK SOCK — I LOVE YOU MORE THAN **EVER**!
I FILLED IT UP WITH TUNA.

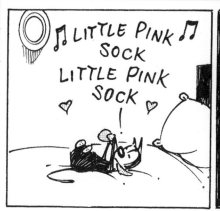

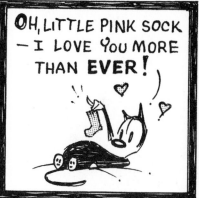

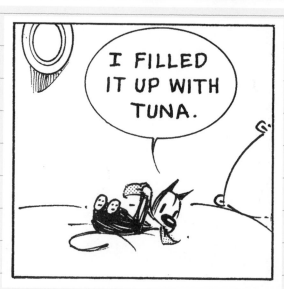

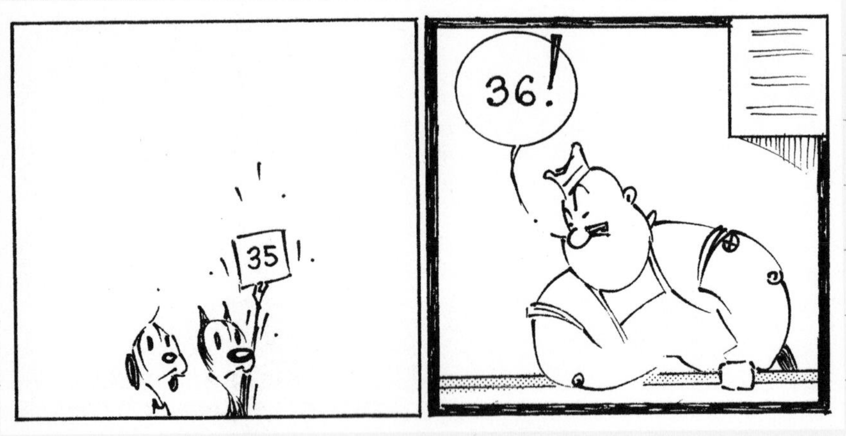
35
36!

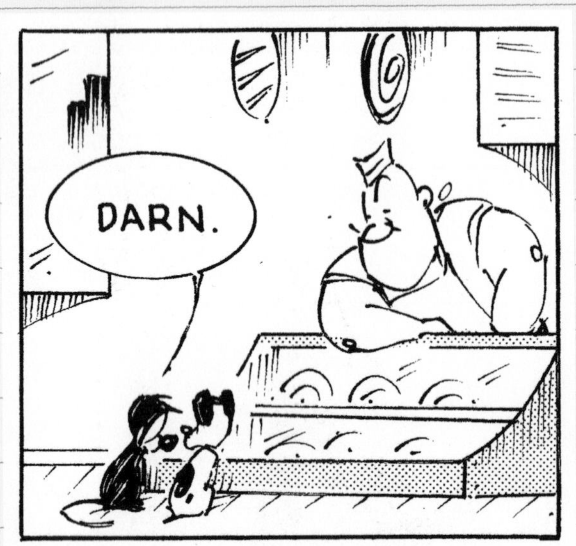
DARN.

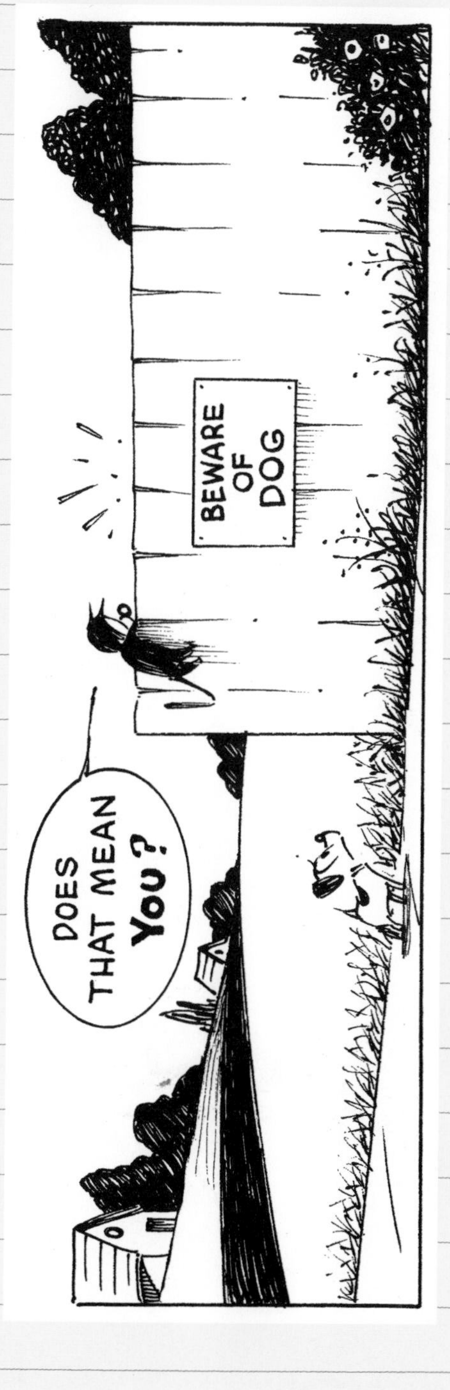
DOES THAT MEAN YOU?
BEWARE OF DOG

Poooo PAK PRAP Poo...
MY PURR NEEDS WORK.

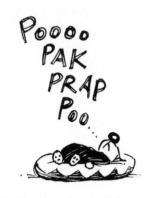

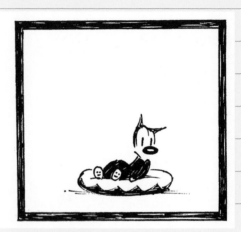

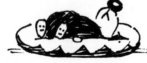

OKAY, EARL, STAY HOME AND BE A GOOD DOG.
THERE GOES MY PIZZA PARTY.

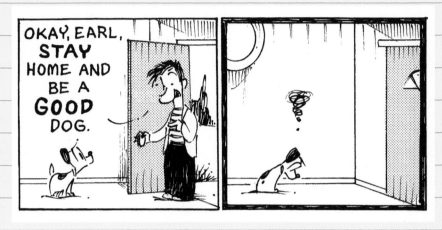

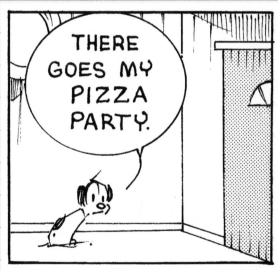

...AND NOW A SONG FOR SPRING!

I PRACTICED ALL WINTER.

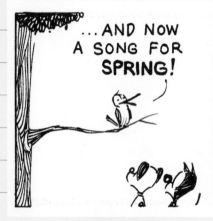

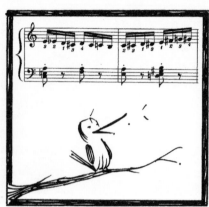

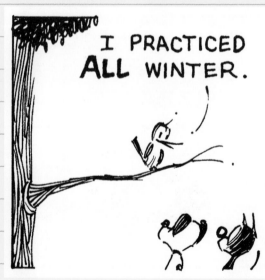

TWEET TWEET TWEET
DUDE...
THAT'S OLD SCHOOL.

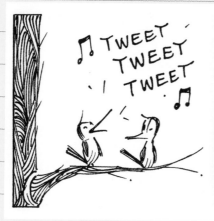

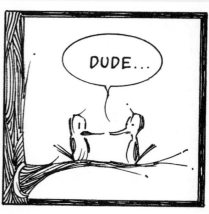

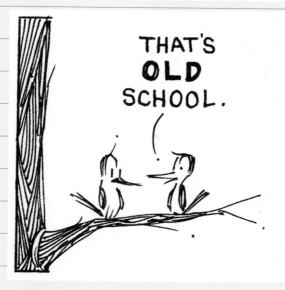

I WROTE A NEW SONG!
A NEW SONG!?! BUT WE'VE BEEN IMPRINTED IN OUR HEARTS TO SING THE SAME SONG FOR THOUSANDS OF GENERATIONS!
YES
BUT
MINE ROCKS!

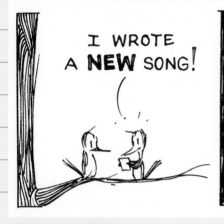

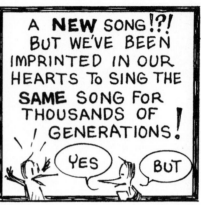

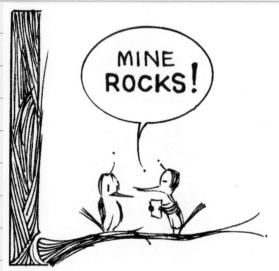

TWEET
TWIX
BRAP.
FOO
TWAP
WEEZ

I HATE KARAOKE NITE.

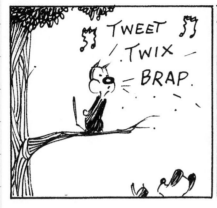

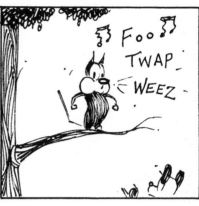

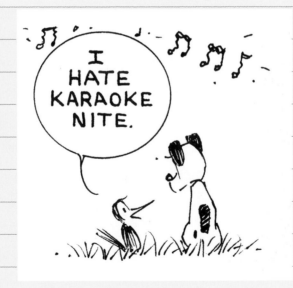

mmmmmmmm
LIFE'S A BREEZE.
YESH.

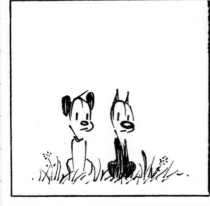

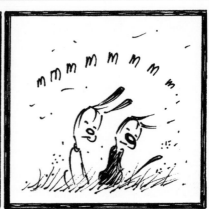

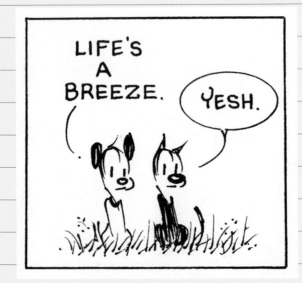

LOOKS LIKE RAIN.
NO, IT DOESN'T.
BAH.

THAT LOOKS LIKE RAIN!

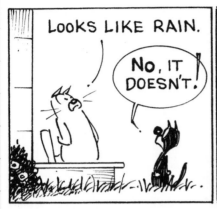

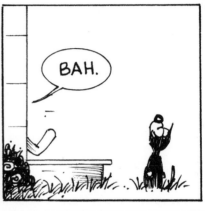

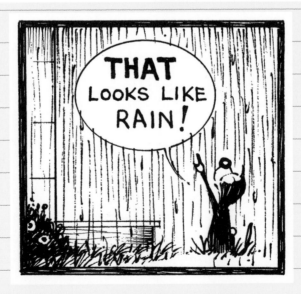

SEE, MOOCH—A LI'L RAIN'S NOT **SO** BAD.
YOU'RE RIGHT
OKAY, EARL

LET'S TRY OUTSIDE.

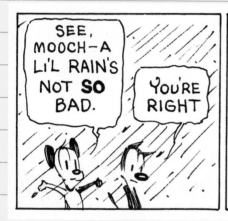

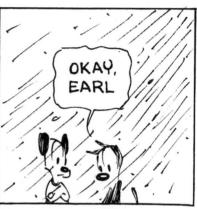

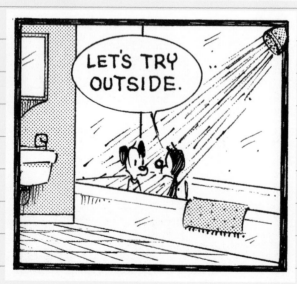

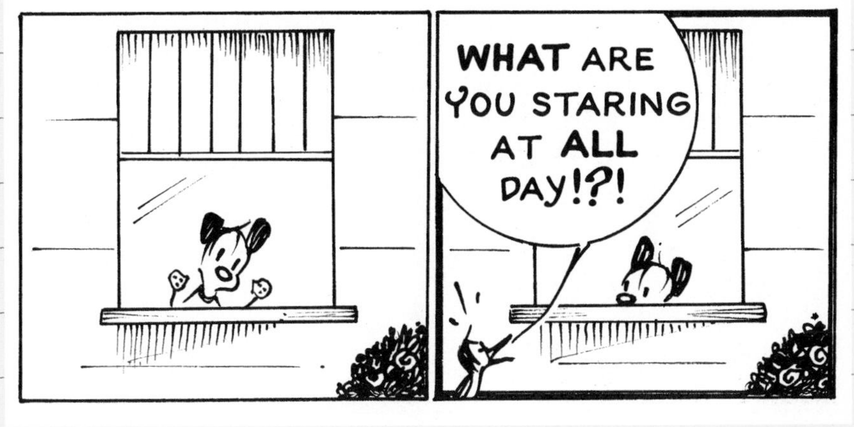
WHAT ARE YOU STARING AT ALL DAY!?!

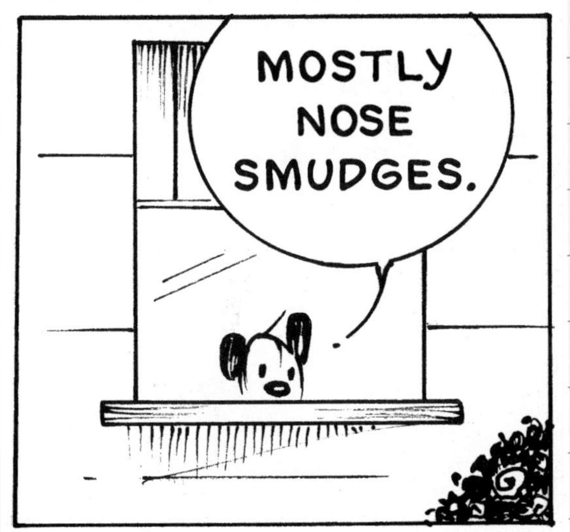
MOSTLY NOSE SMUDGES.

HEY! AREN'T YOU THE GUY WHO PAINTS EGGS, PUTS THEM IN A BASKET AND DELIVERS THEM TO GIRLS AND BOYS?
WHY WOULD I DO THAT !?!

THAT WAS MY NEXT QUESTION.

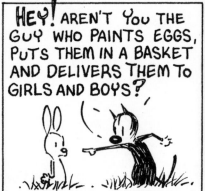

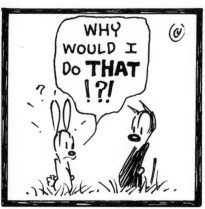

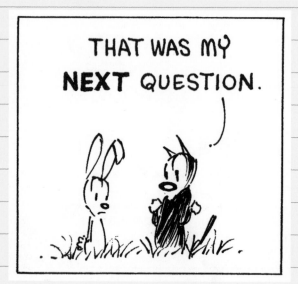

Flowers
Candy
CUTE.
SAY, PAL, THAT MUST BE A FUN JOB.
HA
HA
OH
IT HAS ITS UPS
...AND DOWNS.
GRRRRR

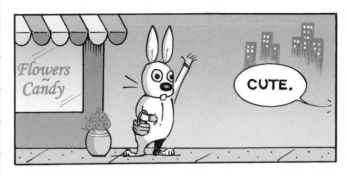

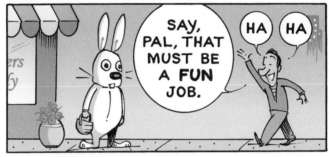

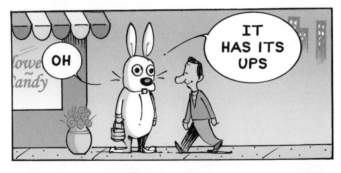

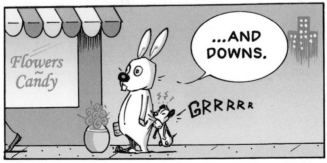

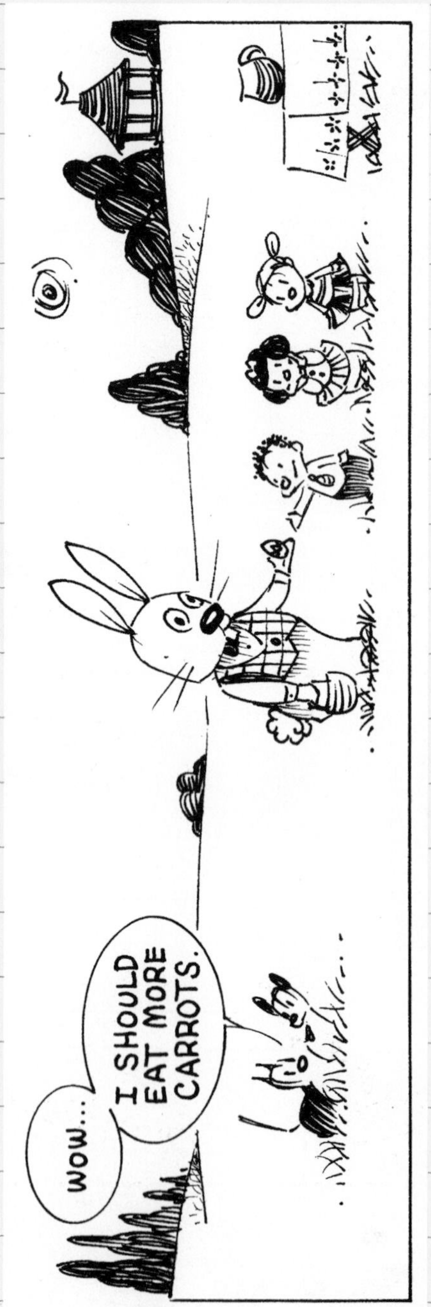
WOW...
I SHOULD EAT MORE CARROTS.

WHAT'CHA DOING, EARL ?
LOOKING FOR A BELLYRUB
IN A FIELD OF CLOVER ?
I THOUGHT I MIGHT GET LUCKY.

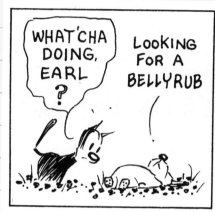

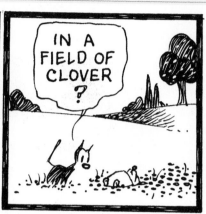

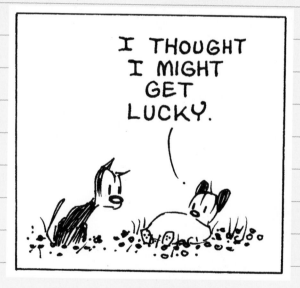

Check Out Receipt

North Point Branch
410-887-7255
www.bcpl.info

Tuesday, August 20, 2024
6:09:45 PM
65416

Item: 31183189719575
Title: BCPL checkout item.
Call no.:
Due: 9/10/2024

Total items: 1

You just saved $35.00 by using
your library today.

Kids can register for
Summer Reading Challenge.
Get a free book and win prizes!
Ask branch staff for details.

HEY, MOOCH! WHAT'CHA DOIN'?
I'M SHMAKING FACES AT THE NEW NEIGHBORS' DOG.
THE NEW NEIGHBORS DON'T HAVE A DOG.
... BUT WE'RE SURE THINKING ABOUT GET-TING ONE.

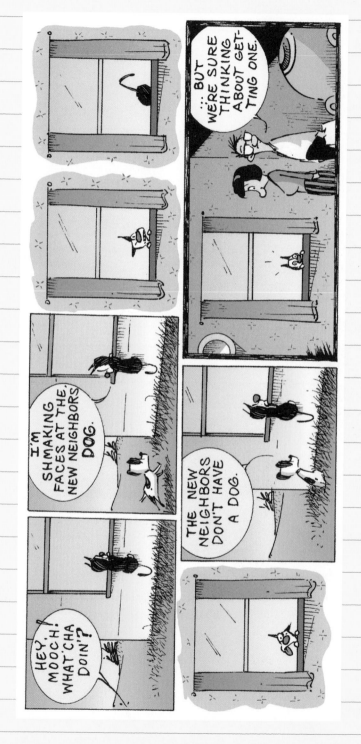

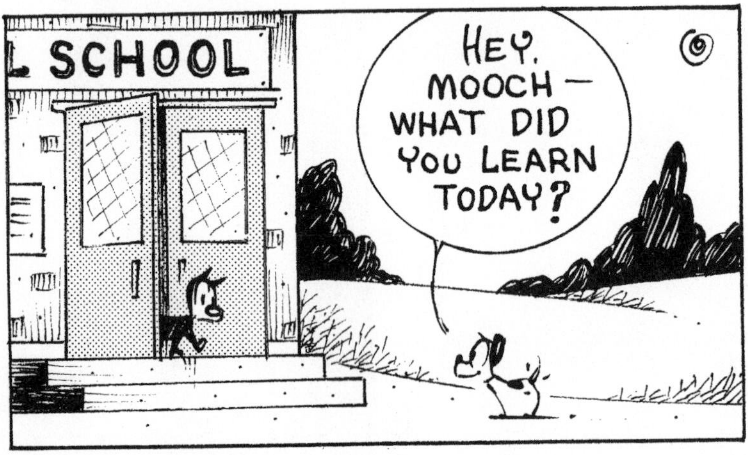
L SCHOOL
HEY,
MOOCH—
WHAT DID
YOU LEARN
TODAY?

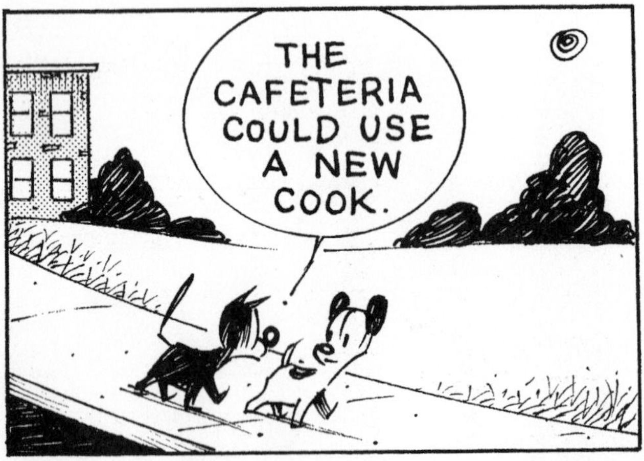
THE
CAFETERIA
COULD USE
A NEW
COOK.

TWEET
TWEET
TWEET
OR SOME-THING LIKE THAT.

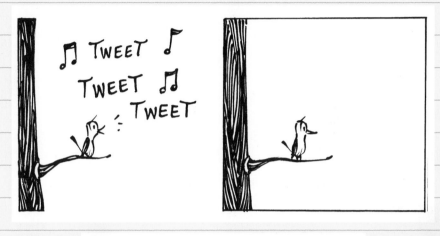

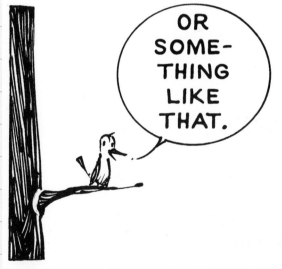

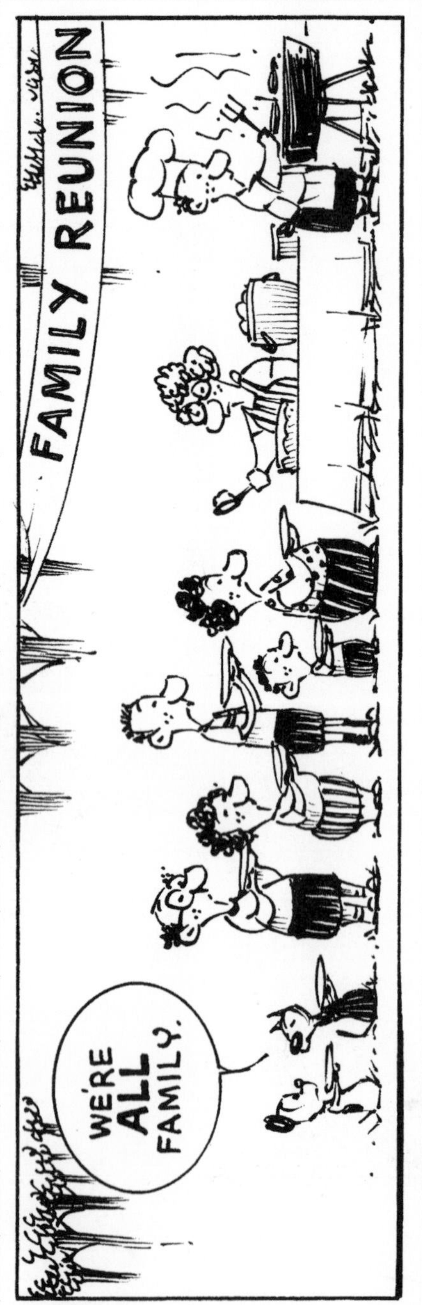
FAMILY REUNION
WE'RE ALL FAMILY.

MEOW.
?
WHAT KIND OF ACCENT WAS THAT!?!

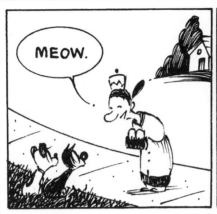

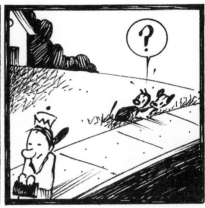

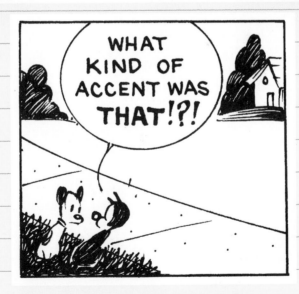

ABCDEFGHI
CAT
... AND WHAT DO CATS SAY ?
MEOW!

12
THE DULL ONES.

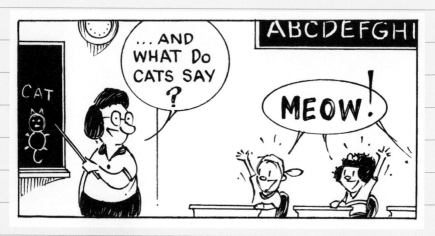

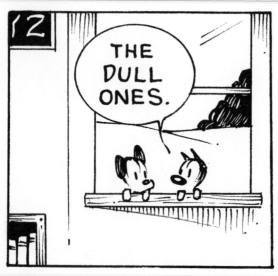

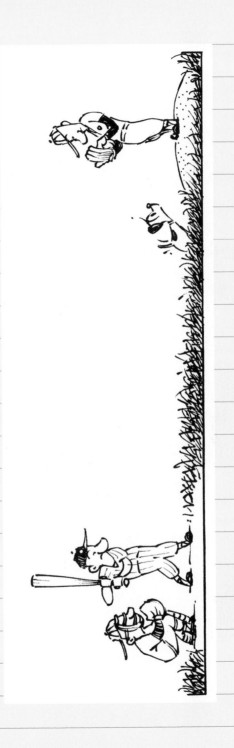

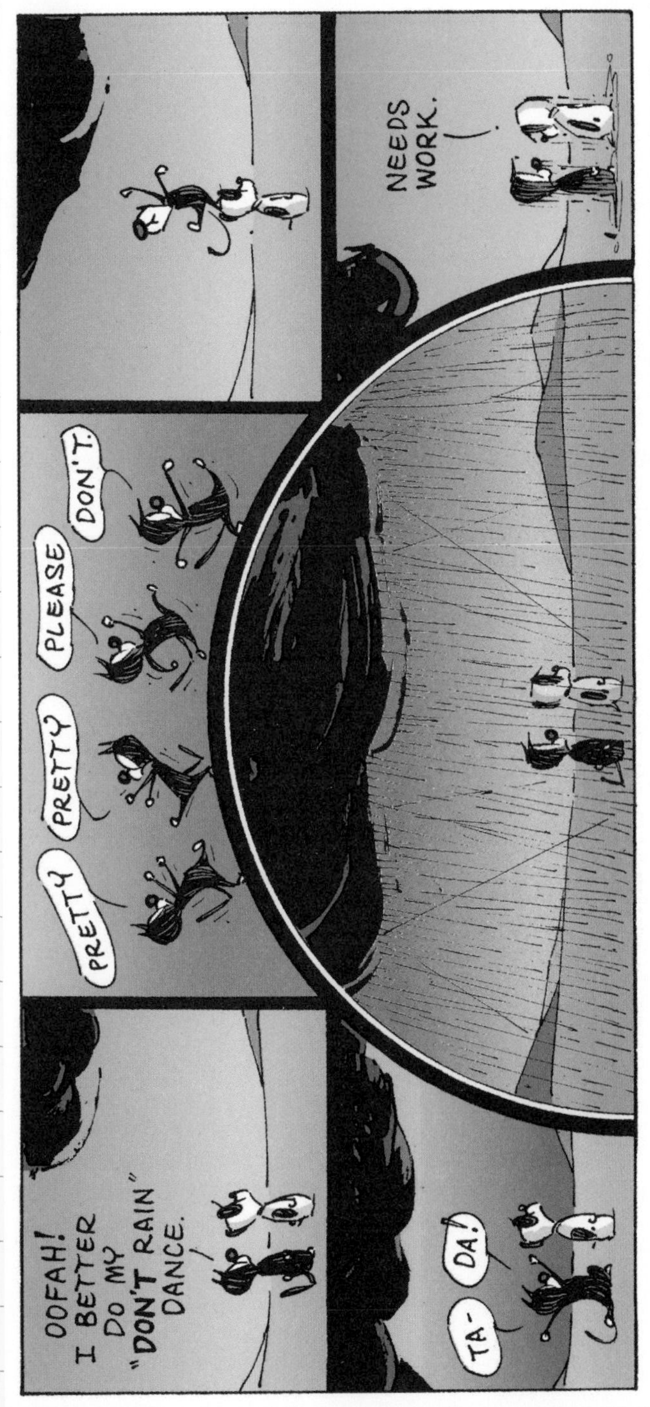
OOFAH! I BETTER DO MY "DON'T RAIN" DANCE.
PRETTY
PRETTY
PLEASE
DON'T.
TA-
DA!
NEEDS WORK.

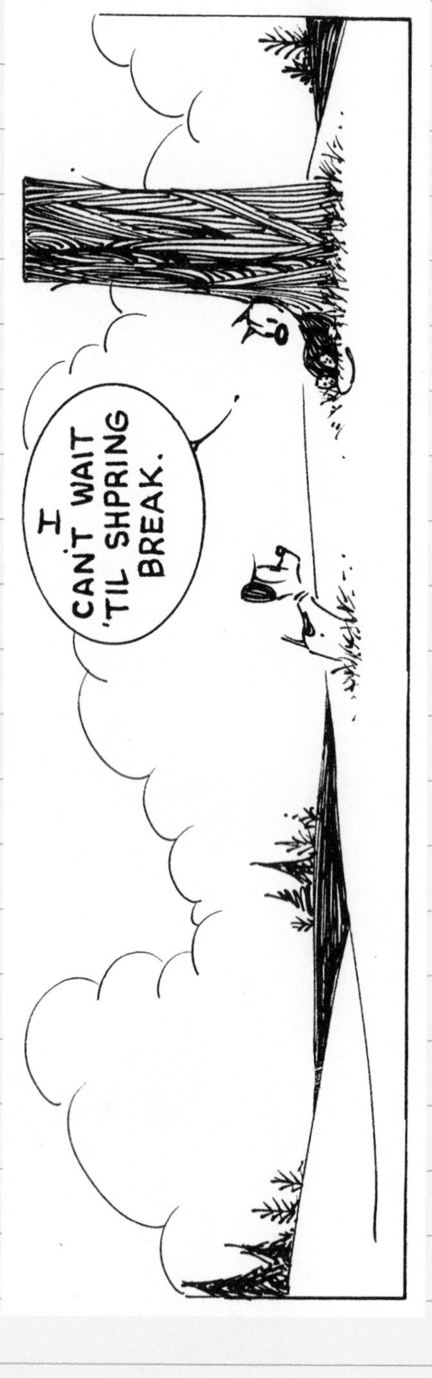
I CAN'T WAIT 'TIL SHPRING BREAK.

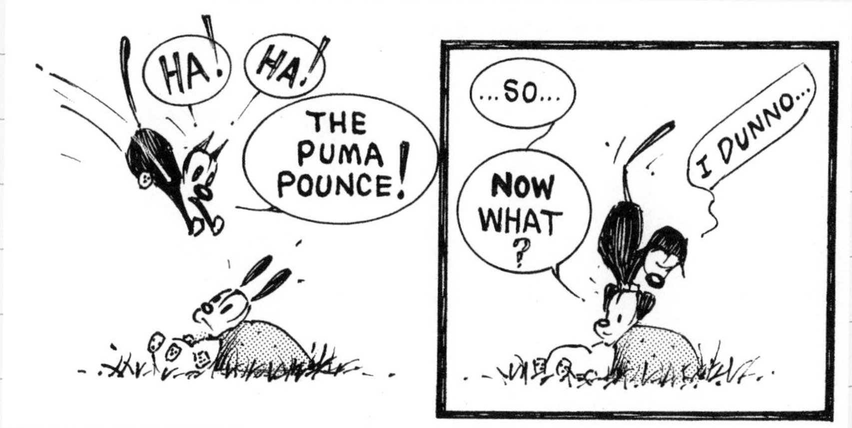
HA! HA!
THE PUMA POUNCE!
...SO...
NOW WHAT?
I DUNNO...

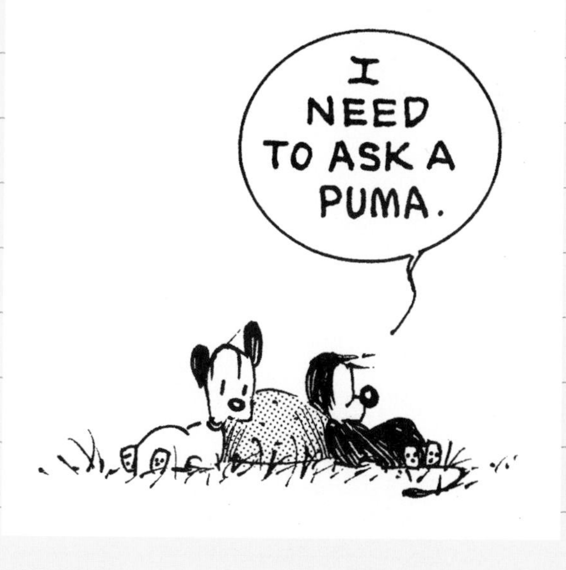
I NEED TO ASK A PUMA.

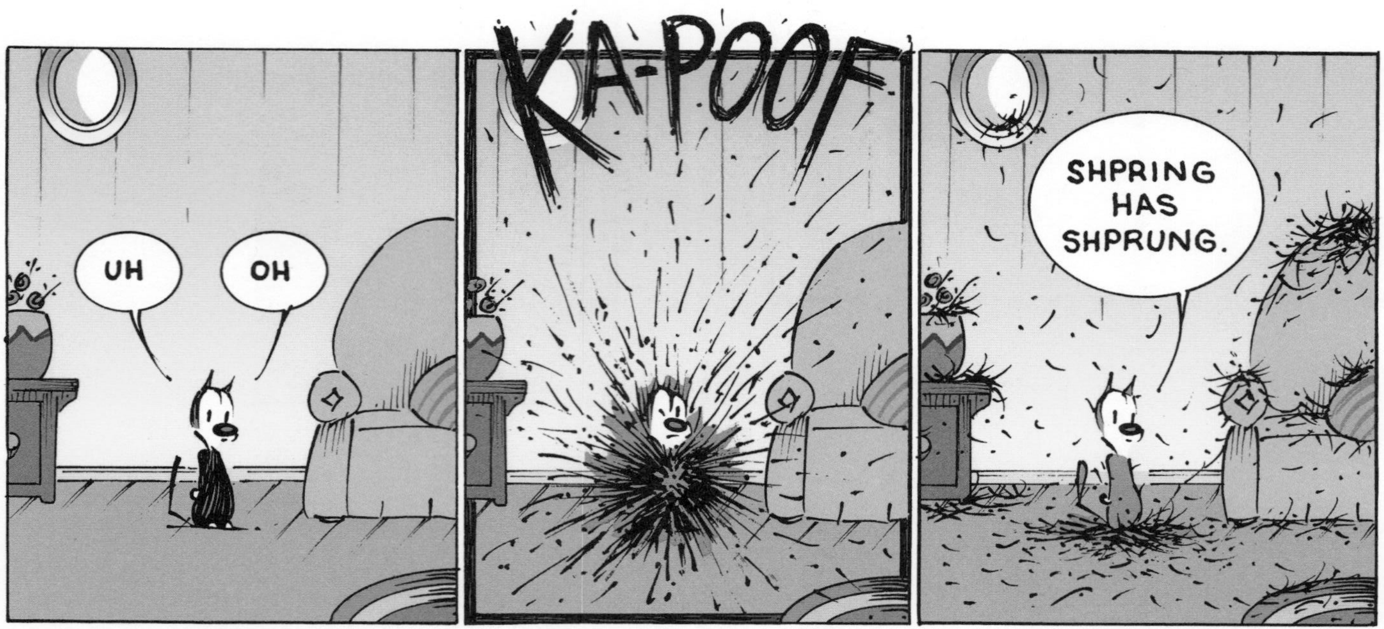
UH
OH
KA-POOF
SHPRING HAS SHPRUNG.

VERY GOOD.
CLAP CLAP
HE NEVER SANG IN PUBLIC BEFORE
CLAP CLAP

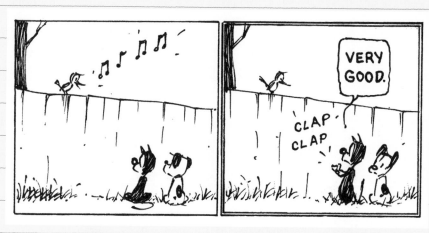

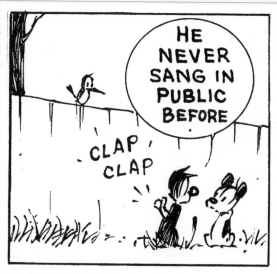

MOOCH'S
TO·DO LIST
1. SHED
DONE.

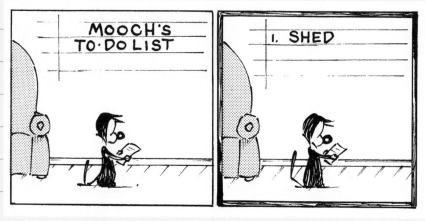

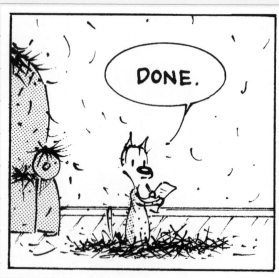

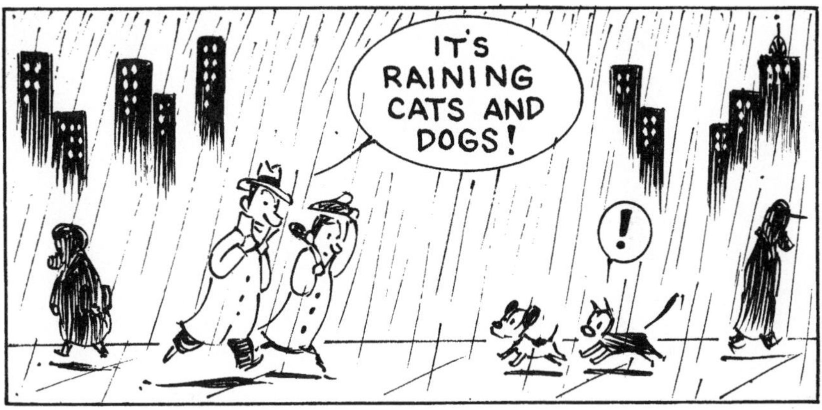
IT'S RAINING CATS AND DOGS!
!

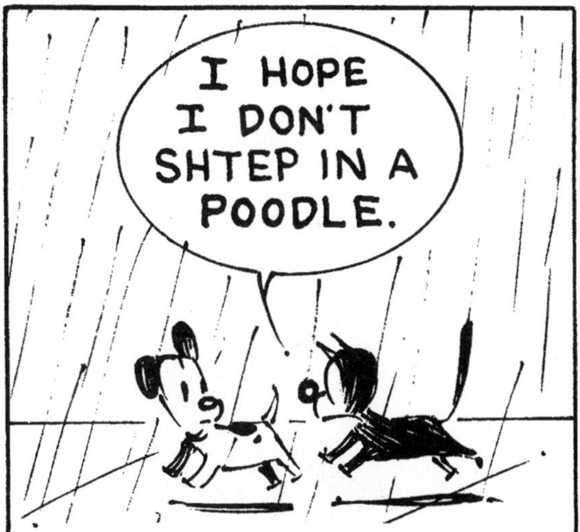
I HOPE I DON'T SHTEP IN A POODLE.

RAIN, RAIN
GO AWAY—
COME AGAIN
SOME OTHER DAY
NOW
TRY IT WITH
FEELING.

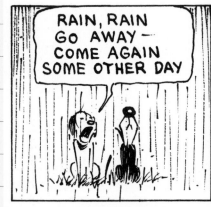

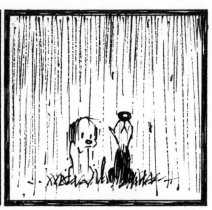

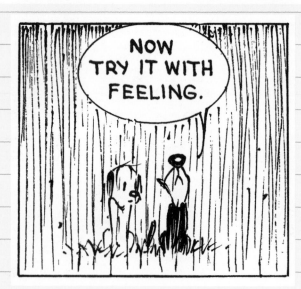

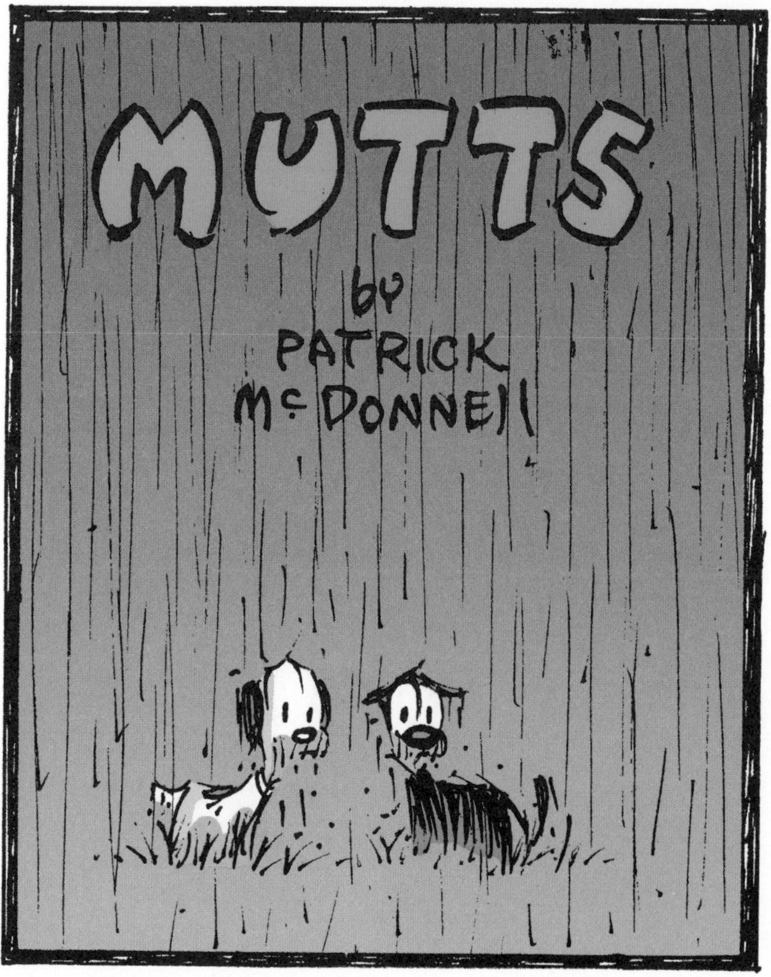
MUTTS
by
PATRICK
McDONNELL

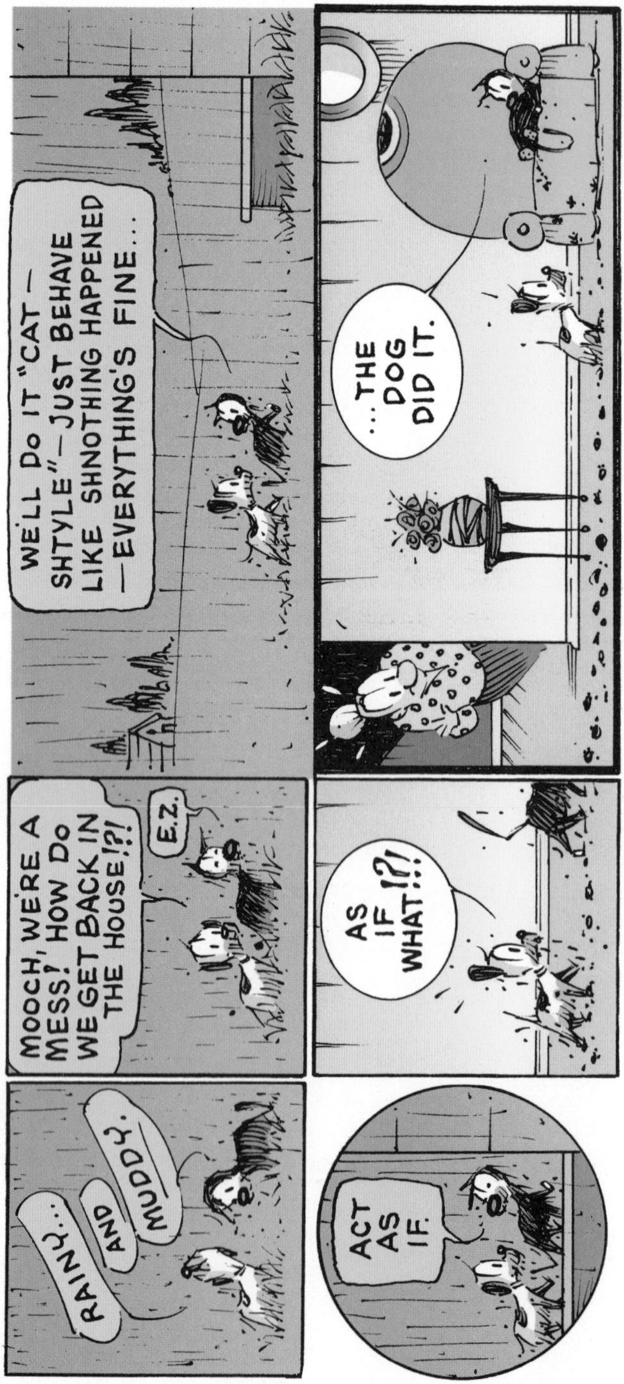
RAINY...
AND
MUDDY.
MOOCH, WE'RE A MESS! HOW DO WE GET BACK IN THE HOUSE!?!
E.Z.
WE'LL DO IT "CAT-SHTYLE"—JUST BEHAVE LIKE SHNOTHING HAPPENED —EVERYTHING'S FINE...
ACT AS IF.
AS IF WHAT!?!
...THE DOG DID IT.

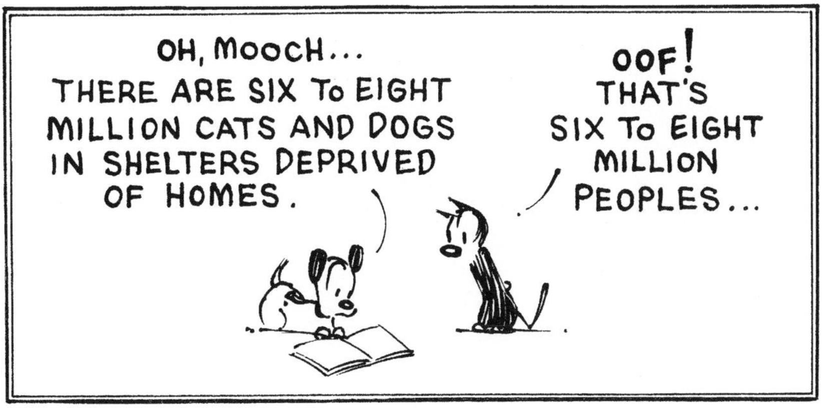
OH, MOOCH...
THERE ARE SIX TO EIGHT MILLION CATS AND DOGS IN SHELTERS DEPRIVED OF HOMES.
OOF! THAT'S SIX TO EIGHT MILLION PEOPLES...

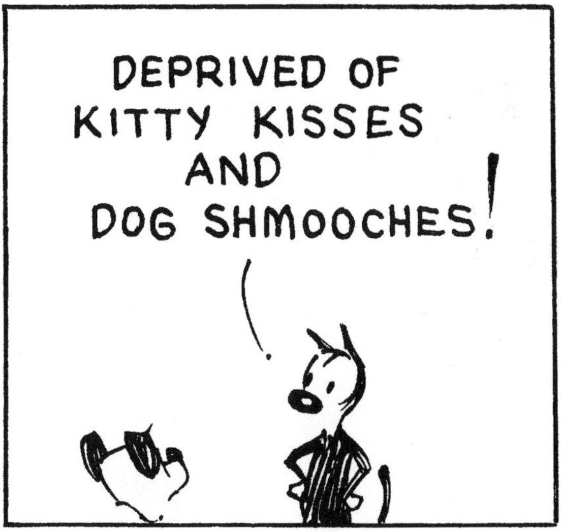
DEPRIVED OF KITTY KISSES AND DOG SHMOOCHES!

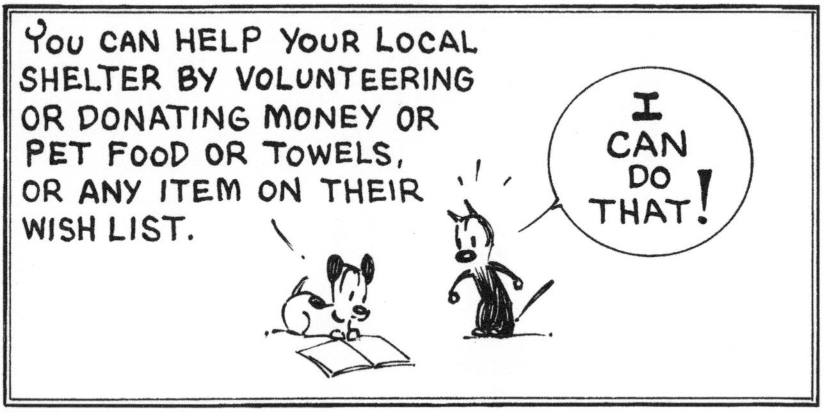
YOU CAN HELP YOUR LOCAL SHELTER BY VOLUNTEERING OR DONATING MONEY OR PET FOOD OR TOWELS, OR ANY ITEM ON THEIR WISH LIST.
I CAN DO THAT!

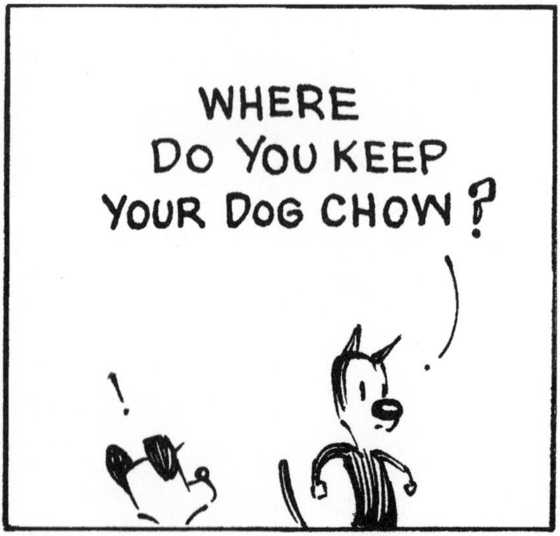
WHERE DO YOU KEEP YOUR DOG CHOW?

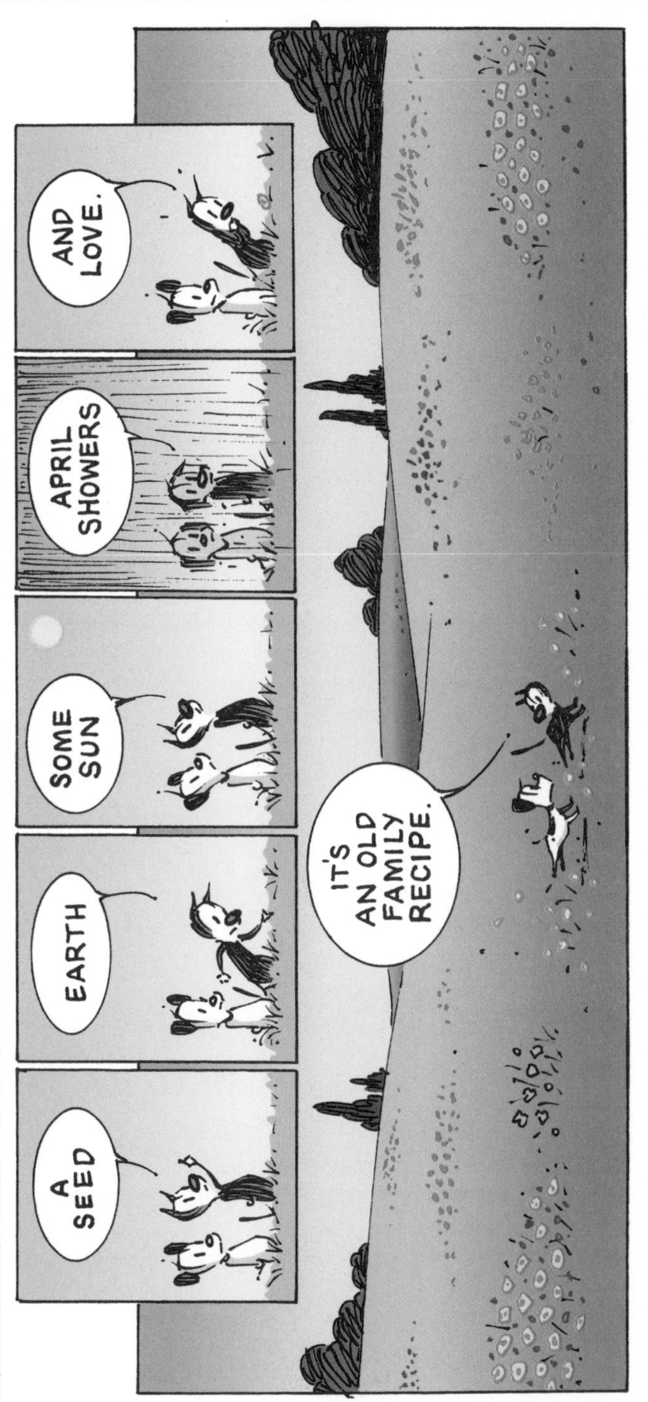
A SEED
EARTH
SOME SUN
APRIL SHOWERS
AND LOVE.
IT'S AN OLD FAMILY RECIPE.

WHAT'S THAT, EARL?
A BIRD HOUSE
OOFAH.
WHO'S THEIR INTERIOR DECORATOR !?!

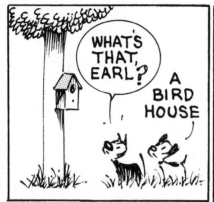

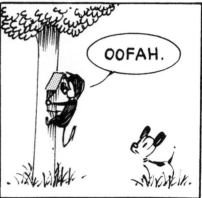

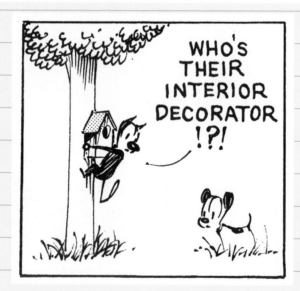

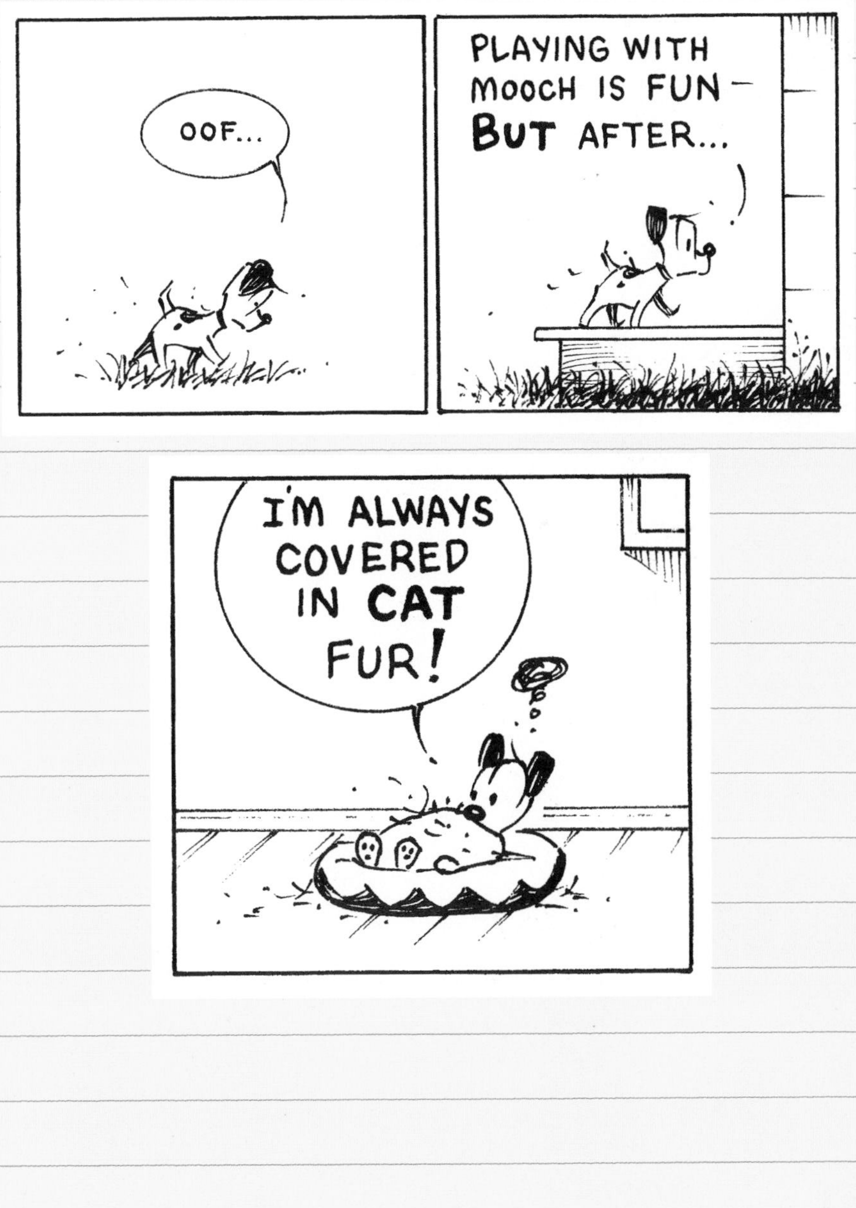
OOF...
PLAYING WITH MOOCH IS FUN— BUT AFTER...
I'M ALWAYS COVERED IN CAT FUR!

AUGH... MOOCH, I ATE SOMETHING THAT DISAGREED WITH ME...
GURGLE
WEE OOOOG
GURGLE
SOUNDS LIKE IT'S SHTILL COMPLAINING

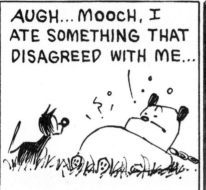

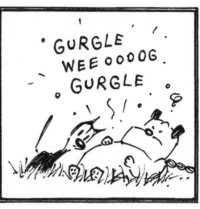

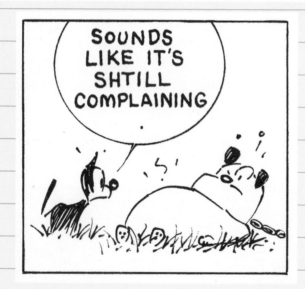

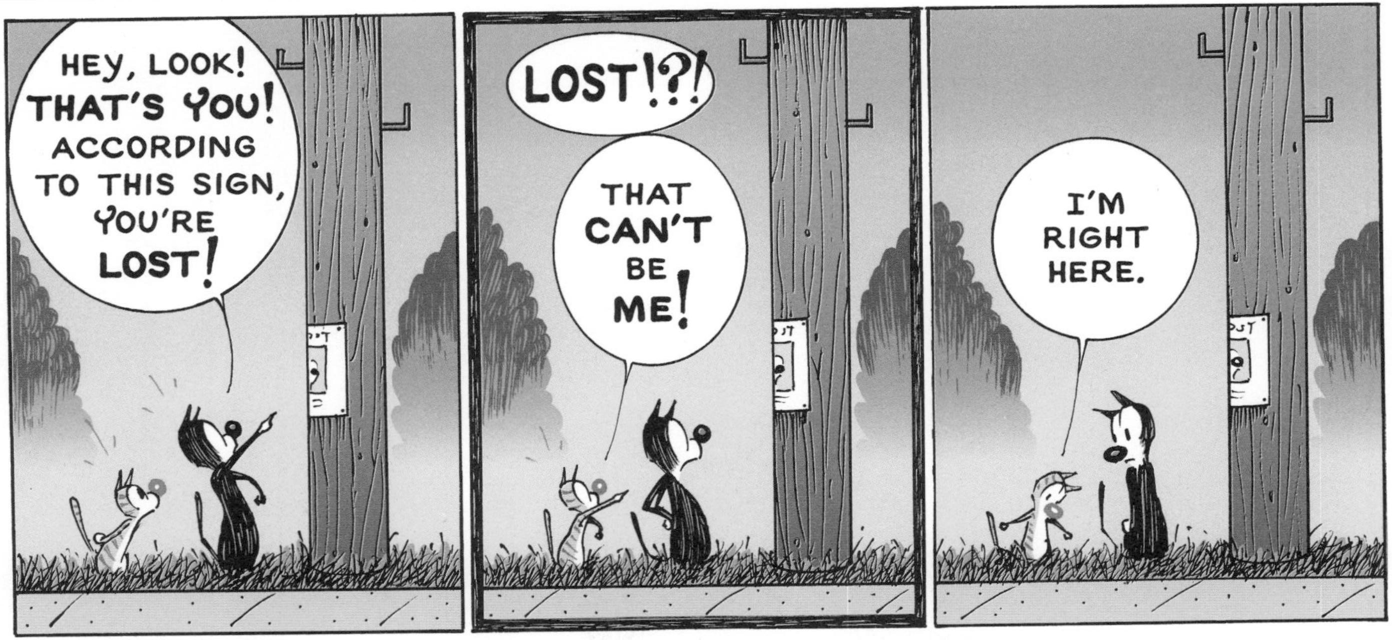
HEY, LOOK! THAT'S YOU! ACCORDING TO THIS SIGN, YOU'RE LOST!
LOST!?!
THAT CAN'T BE ME!
I'M RIGHT HERE.

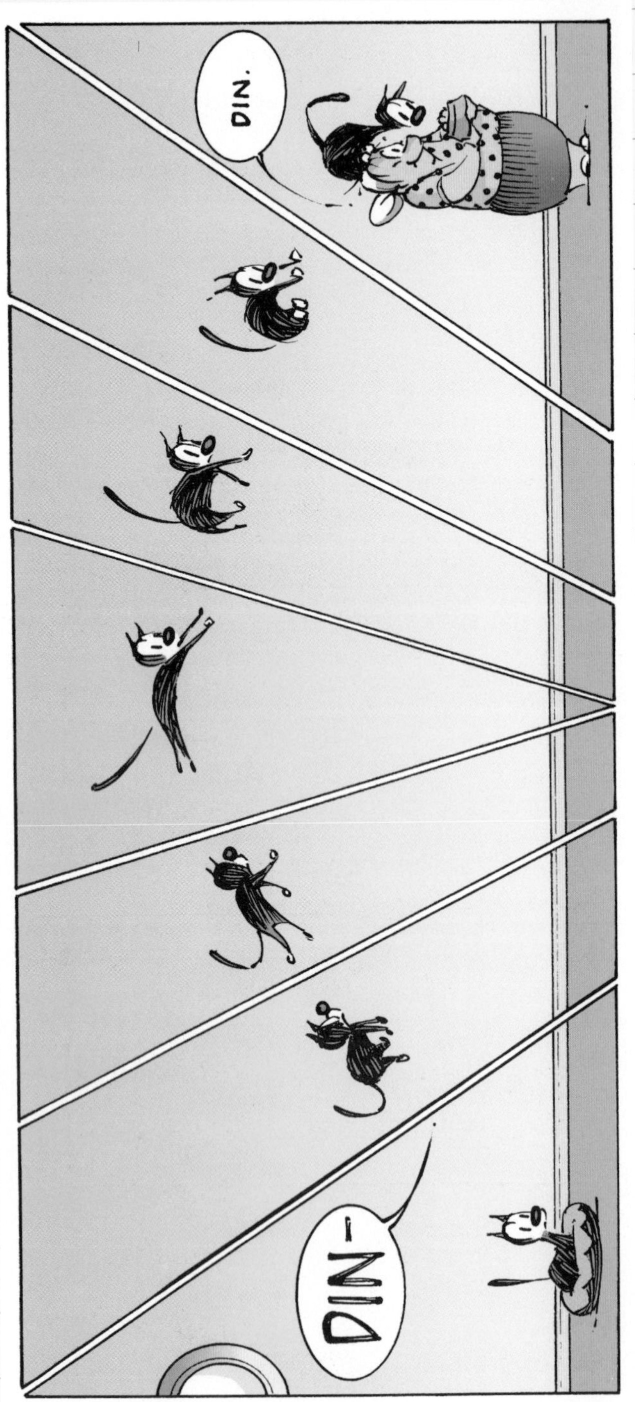
DIN-
DIN.

MOOCH— THAT'S A CATER-PILLAR
A CAT-ERPILLAR !?!
ARE WE RELATED?
HE SAYS MY TAIL LOOKS LIKE HIS UNCLE BENNY.

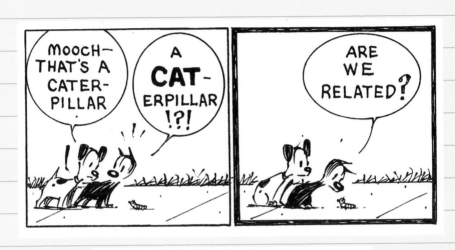

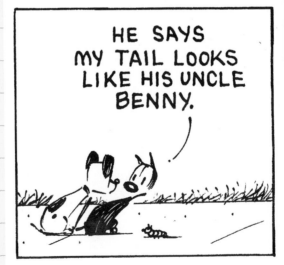

THIS CATERPILLAR SAYS HE'S GOING TO TURN INTO A BUTTERFLY!!!
YESH!
AND I'M GOING TO TURN INTO A HANDSOME PRINCE, AND EARL INTO A LI'L DAFFODIL!

TWO CAN PLAY AT THAT GAME.

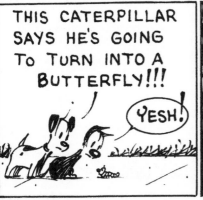

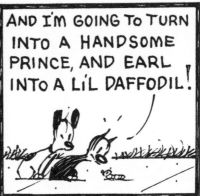

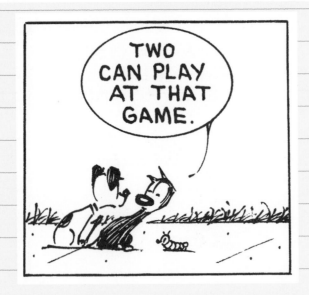

MOOCH, THIS CATERPILLAR SAYS HE'S GOING TO TURN INTO A BUTTERFLY.
...WELL...
WE'RE WAITING.

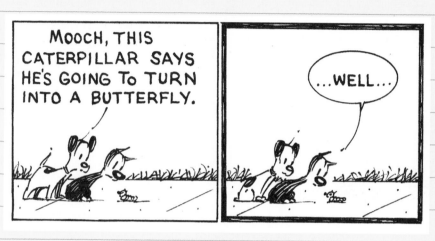

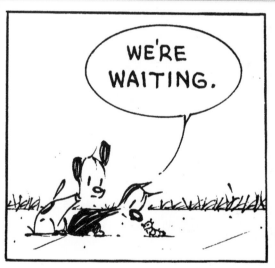

MOOCH, THAT FUZZY LI'L CATERPILLAR REALLY **DOES** TURN INTO A BEAUTIFUL BUTTERFLY!
YOU JUST BLEW MY MIND.

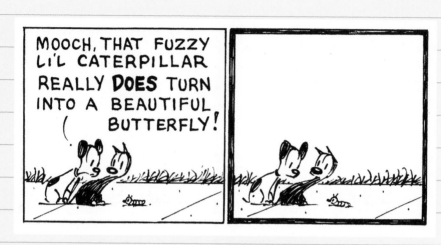

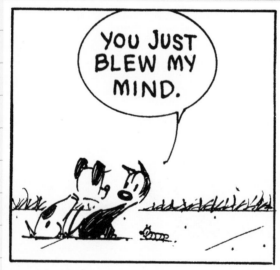

SO IF SOMEDAY OUR CATERPILLAR FRIEND TURNS INTO A BUTTER-FLY, HOW WILL WE RECOGNIZE HIM!?!
BY HIS SMILE.

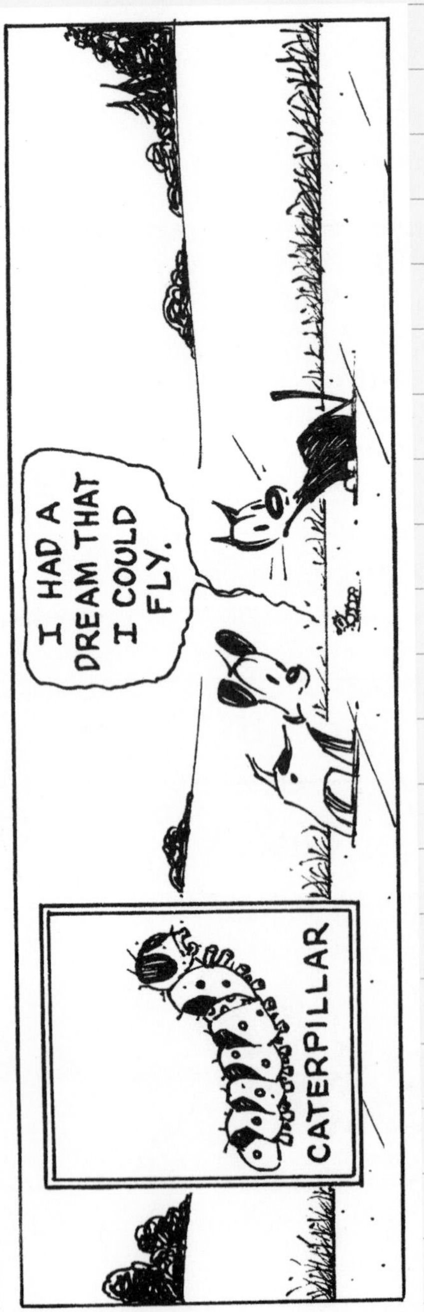
CATERPILLAR
I HAD A DREAM THAT I COULD FLY.

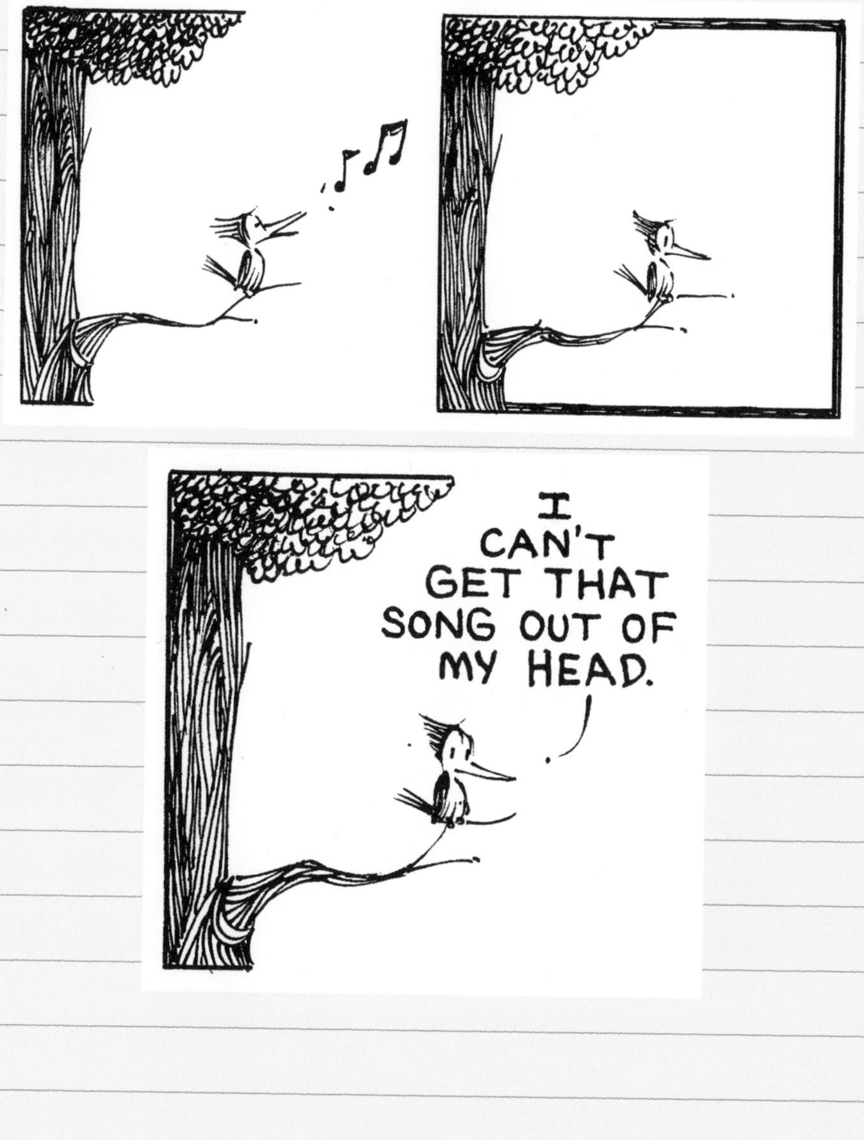
I CAN'T GET THAT SONG OUT OF MY HEAD.

OINK
VENI VIDI OINKI
PIG LATIN.

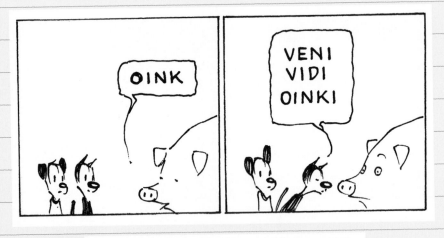

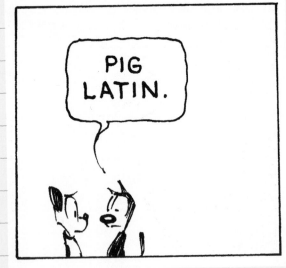

CLUCK CLUCK BOCK-A BOCK-A
BOCK-A BOCK BOCK-A CLUCK CLUCK
PARDON THE FOWL LANGUAGE.

MOO.
MOOOUUU
SHE'S MILKING IT.

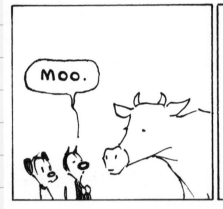

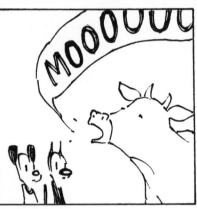

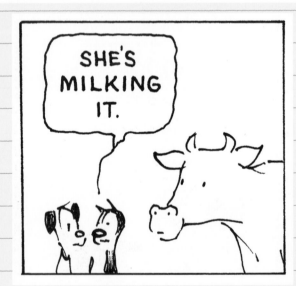

GOBBLE GOBBLE
GOBBLE GOBBLE GOBBLE GOBBLE GOBBLE
THAT WAS A LOT TO SHWALLOW.

QUACK
QUACK
QUACK
QUACK
QUACK
QUACK
QUACK
QUACK
QUACK
QUACK
QUACK
QUACK
QUACK
QUACK
QUACK
QUACK

THAT THEORY WAS A LITTLE QUACKY.

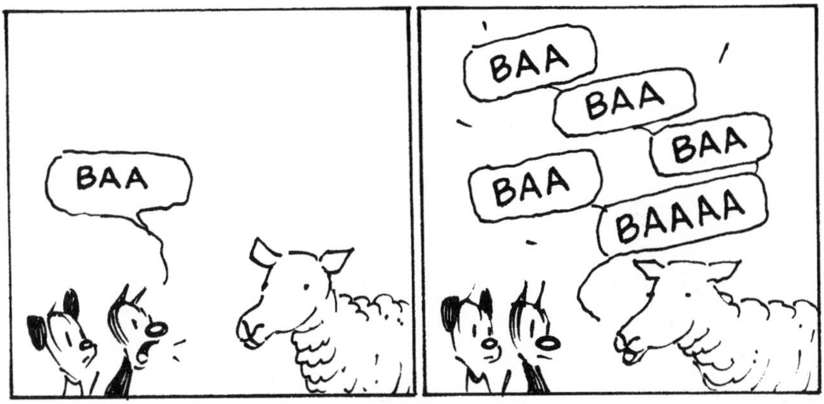
BAA
BAA
BAA
BAA
BAA
BAAAA

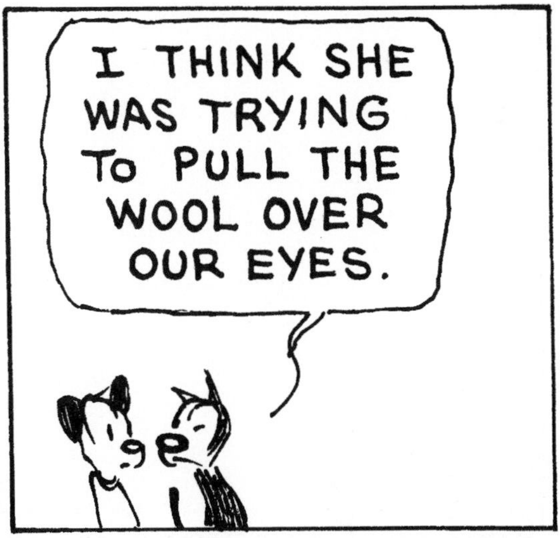
I THINK SHE WAS TRYING TO PULL THE WOOL OVER OUR EYES.

ELEPHANT.
PINK SOCK.
FISH.
CLOUD.
FINALLY!

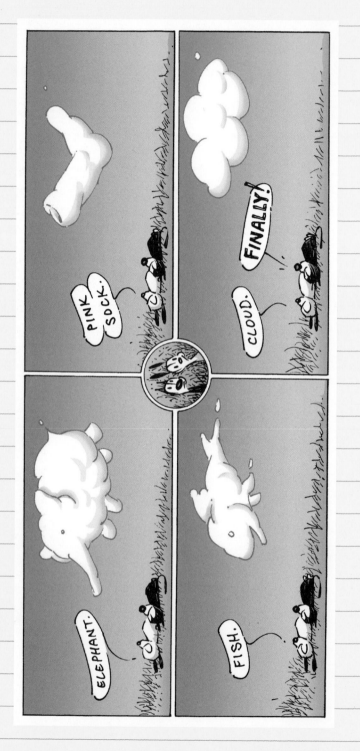

THE MIGHTY SHPHINX SEES ALL • KNOWS ALL
TELL ME, OH MIGHTY SHPHINX, HOW DID YOU FIND THE WEATHER IN EGYPT?
I JUST WENT OUTSIDE AND— THERE IT WAS.

OH, ALL-KNOWING SHPHINX, YOU'VE GOT TO HELP ME.
YESH.
EVERYONE THINKS I'M A LIAR!
I FIND THAT HARD TO BELIEVE.

TELL ME, ALL-KNOWING SHPHINX – WHAT IS MY PROBLEM?
YOU WILL NEVER SHMAKE ANY PROGRESS UNTIL YOU GET OVER ALL YOUR PHOBIAS!
I WAS AFRAID YOU'D SAY THAT.

OH, MIGHTY SHPHINX, WHAT IS YOUR ADVICE?
THE BEST THING FOR YOU TO DO IS TO GIVE UP **ALL** SHWEETS AND LATE-NITE PARTYING.

WHAT'S SECOND BEST?

OH, SHPHINX, CAN YOU TEACH ME TO DO YOGA?
HOW FLEXIBLE ARE YOU?
WELL, I CAN'T DO FRIDAYS.

OH, MIGHTY SHPHINX, **TELL** ME, HAVE YOU LIVED HERE **ALL** YOUR LIFE?
NOT YET.

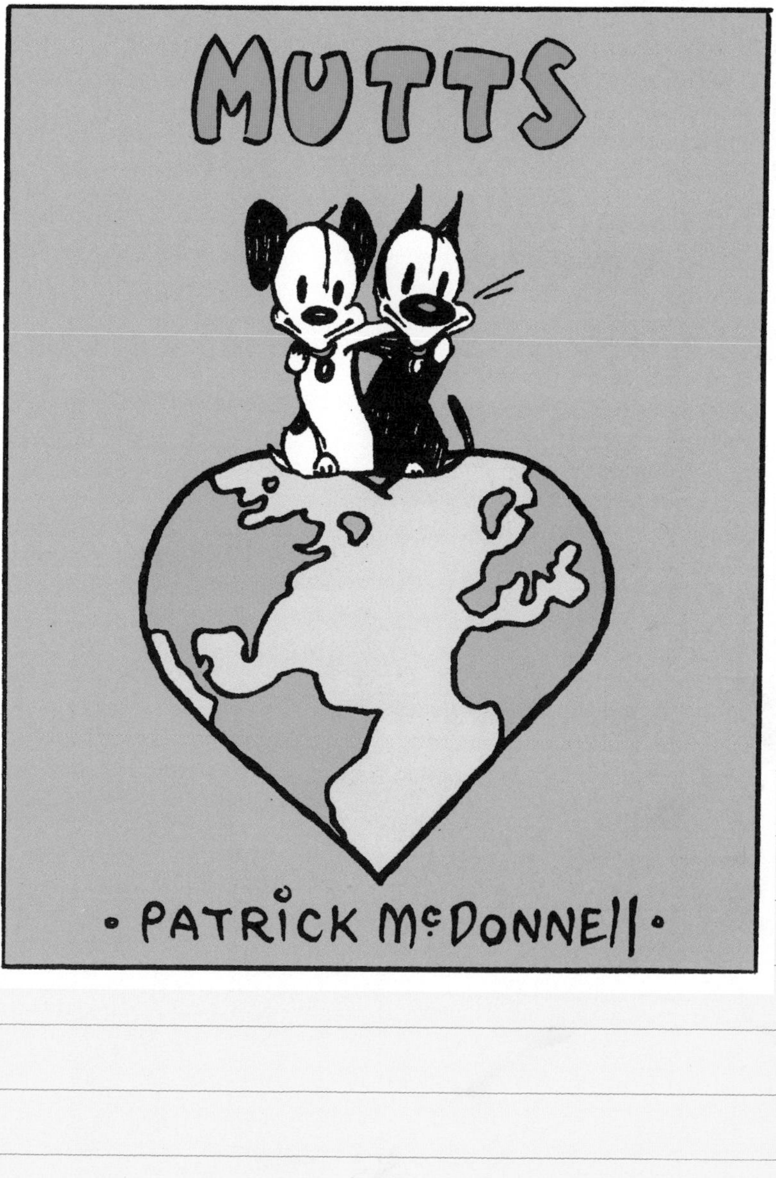
MUTTS
• PATRICK McDONNELL •

The Earth is what we all have in common.

– Wendell Berry

OH, YOU POOR, POOR THING. TIED UP IN CHAINS ALL DAY.
WOULD YOU LIKE SOME OF MY SCHOOL LUNCH?
I'M IN LOVE.

OH, HERE COMES THAT GIRL WHO TREATS ME SO KINDLY.
WAG
WAG WAG
OH
MY.
I THOUGHT I FORGOT HOW TO DO THAT.

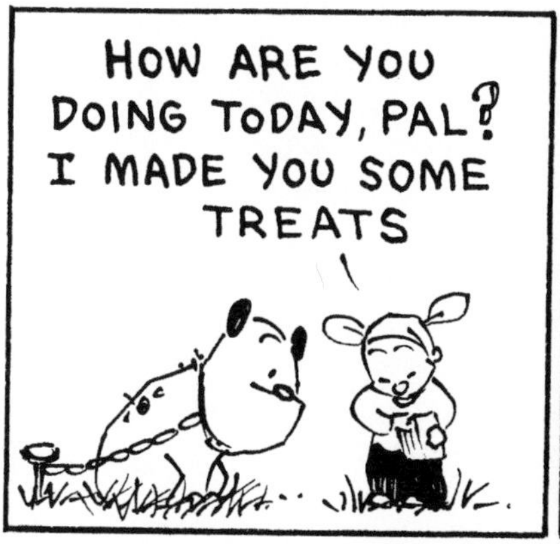
HOW ARE YOU DOING TODAY, PAL? I MADE YOU SOME TREATS

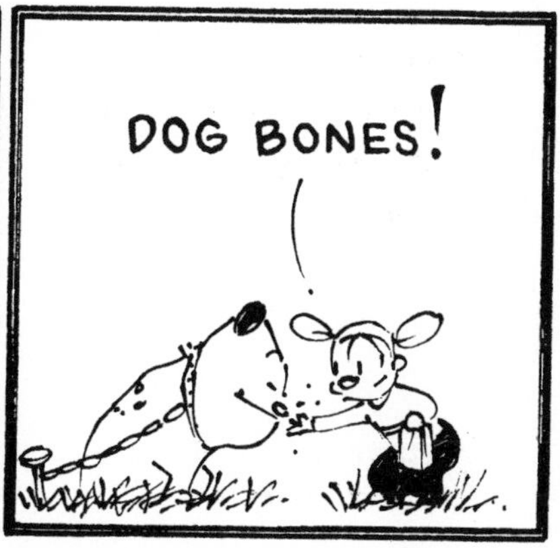
DOG BONES!

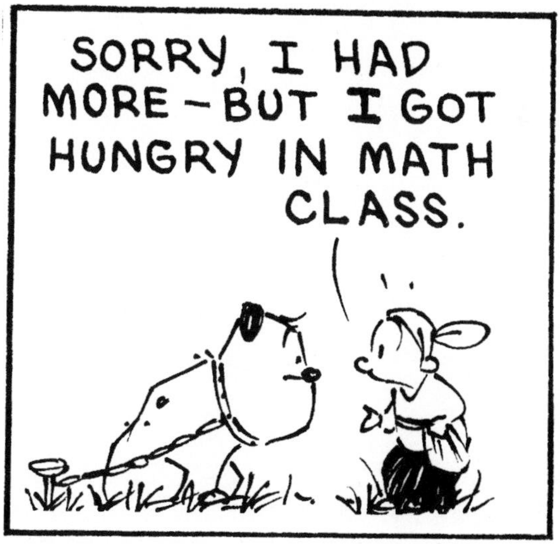
SORRY, I HAD MORE—BUT I GOT HUNGRY IN MATH CLASS.

TIED UP ALL THE TIME AND YOU ARE STILL A **SWEETIE** — I DON'T KNOW HOW YOU DO IT!
THE CHAINS AROUND MY NECK

NOT MY HEART.

OKAY, PAL, I HAVE TO GO TO SCHOOL NOW ~ BUT I HOPE TO SEE YOU SOON.
DON'T WORRY

I'LL BE HERE.

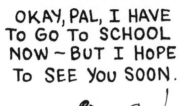

GEE...
I'M NOT MUCH
OF A WATCHDOG
ANYMORE...
NOW I'M JUST
WATCHING
TIME GO BY...
UNTIL
THAT SWEET GIRL
COMES BACK.

I'VE NEVER SEEN A BUTTERFLY IN A HURRY.

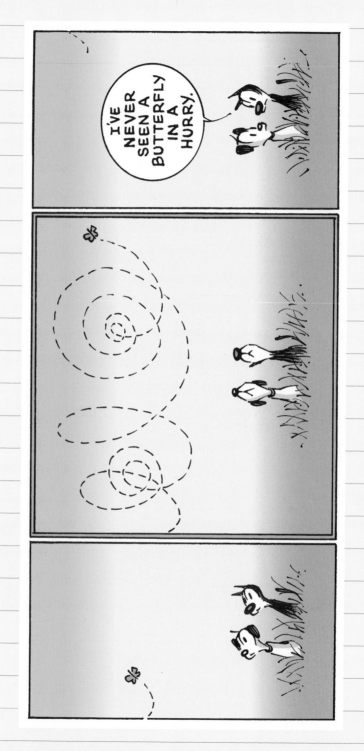

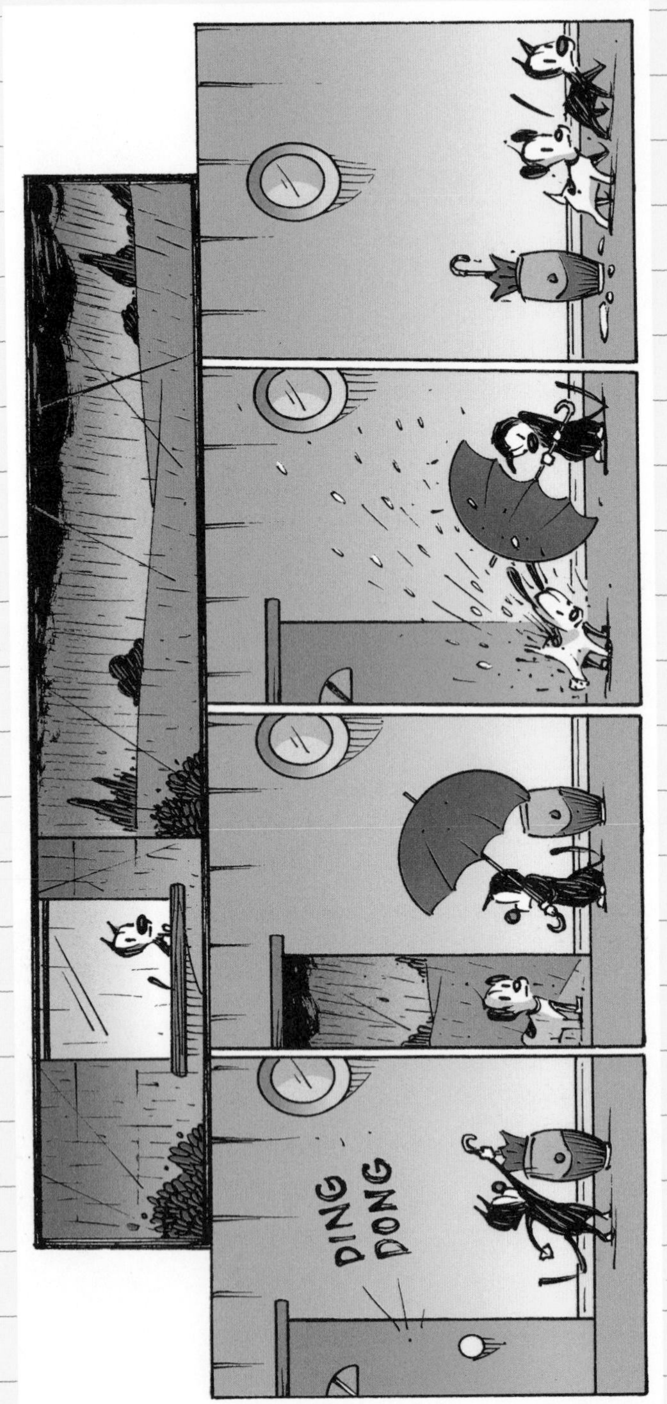
DING DONG

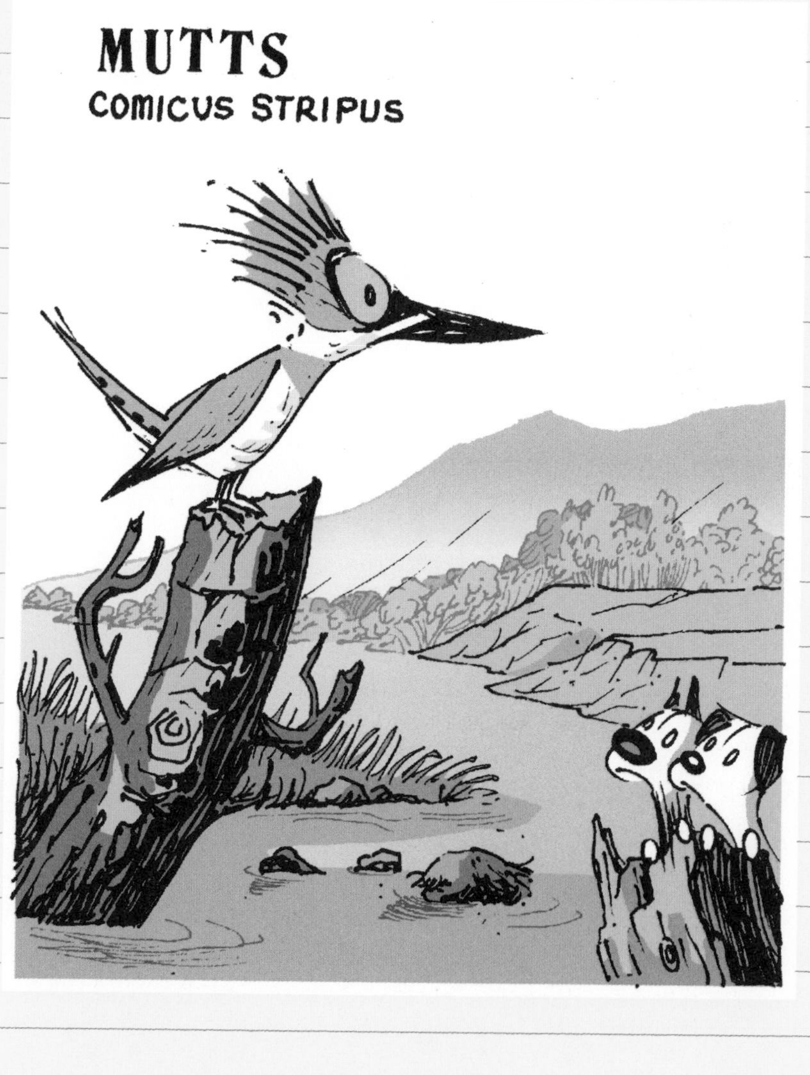
MUTTS
COMICUS STRIPUS

I WROTE THAT FOR YOU.

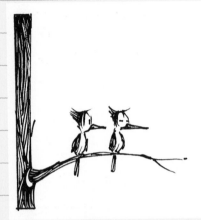

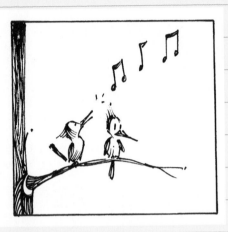

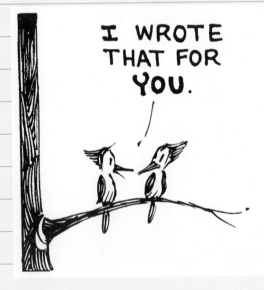

HEY, MOOCH
IT'S SPRING!
SO I HEAR.

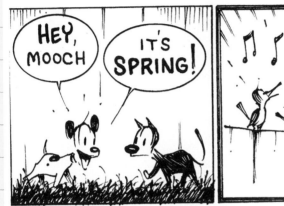

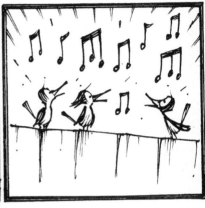

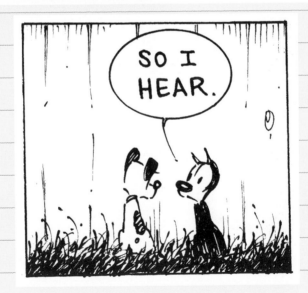

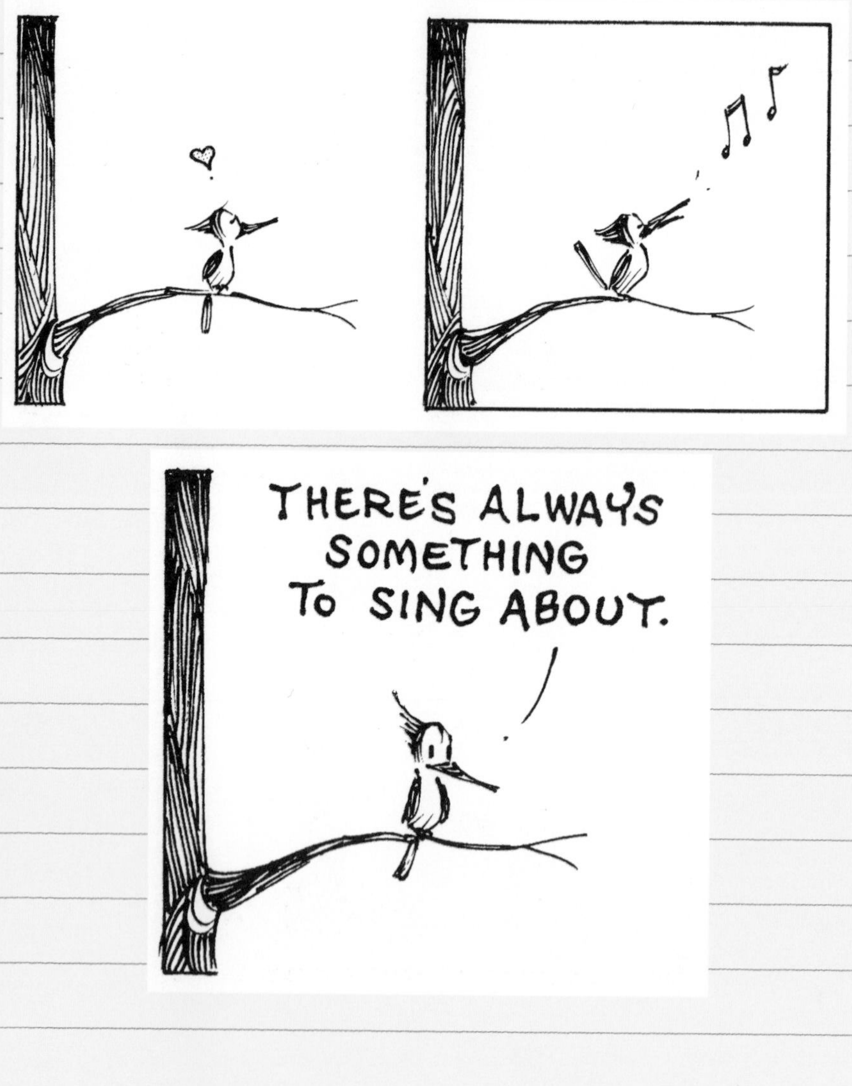
THERE'S ALWAYS SOMETHING TO SING ABOUT.

DOGGY COMIX
by EARL
SPEAK!
ARF

"MEOW" WOULD HAVE BEEN FUNNIER.

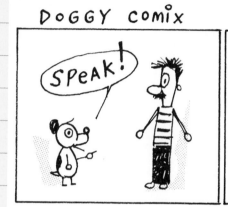

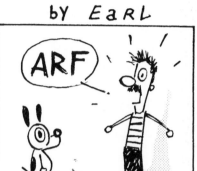

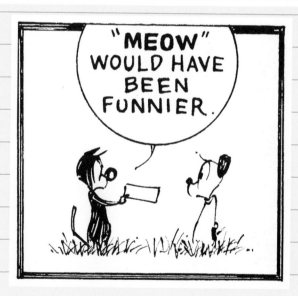

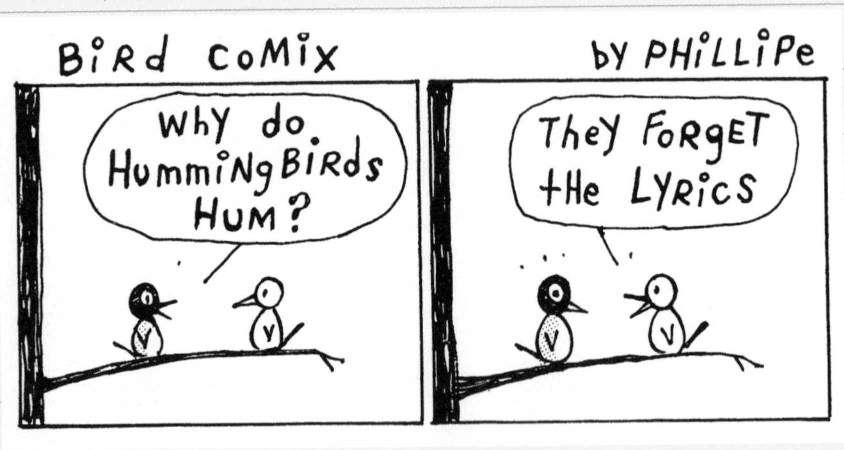
BiRd CoMiX
by PHiLLiPe
Why do HummiNgBiRds Hum?
They ForgeT tHe LYRicS

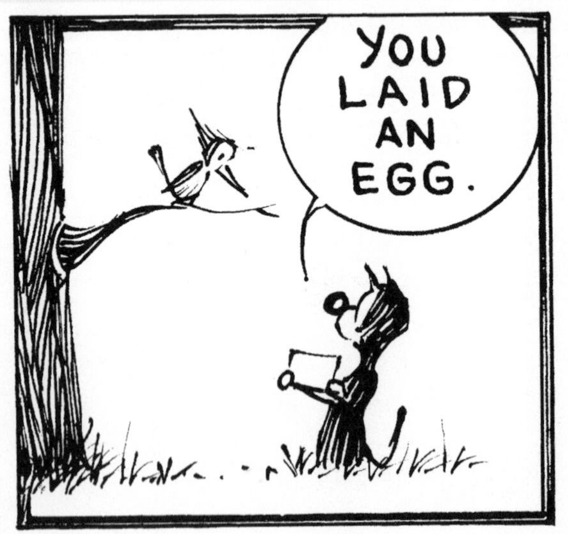
YOU LAID AN EGG.

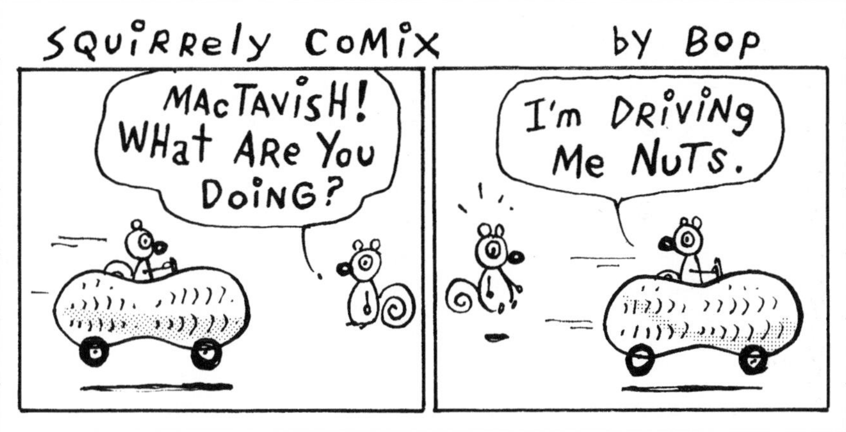
SQUIRRELY COMIX
by BOP
MACTAVISH! WHAT ARE YOU DOING?
I'M DRIVING ME NUTS.

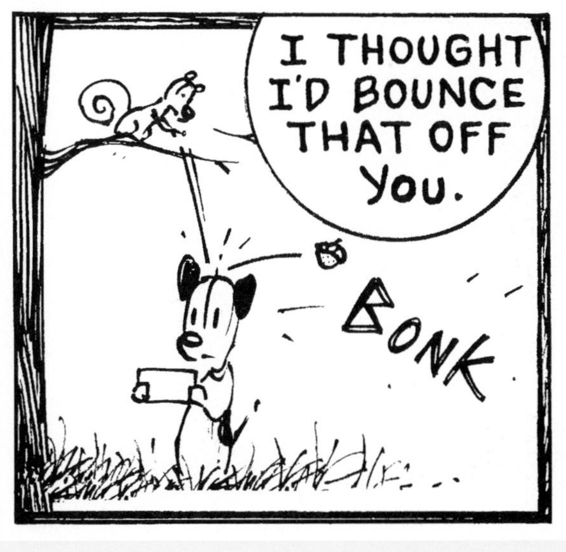
I THOUGHT I'D BOUNCE THAT OFF YOU.
BONK

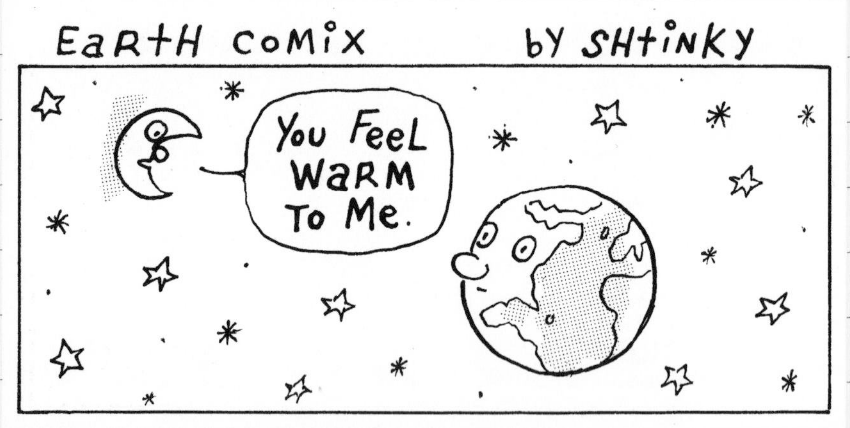
EaRtH coMix
by SHtinKY
You FeeL WaRM To Me.

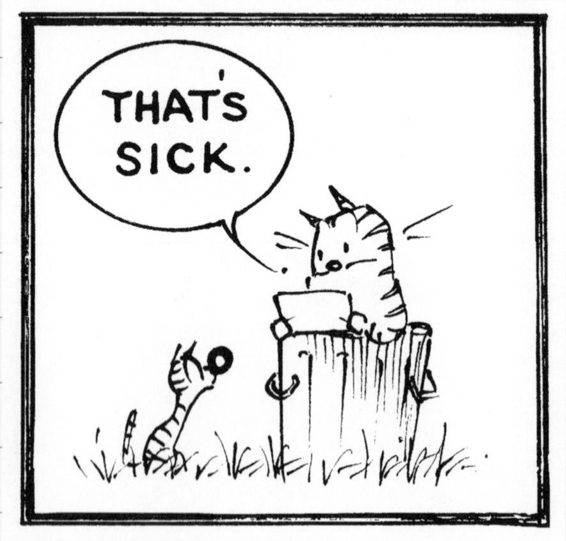
THAT'S SICK.

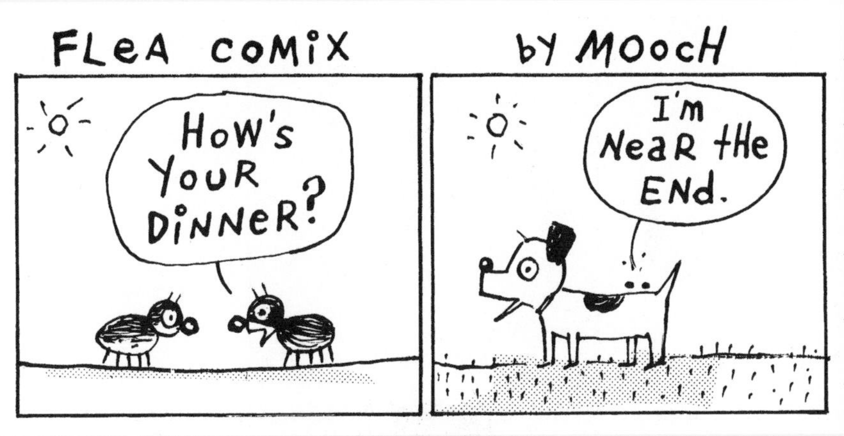
FLEA COMIX
by MOOCH
HOW'S YOUR DINNER?
I'M NEAR THE END.

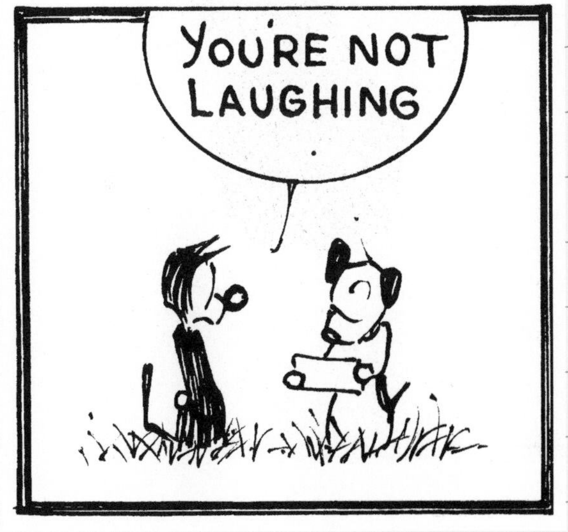
YOU'RE NOT LAUGHING.

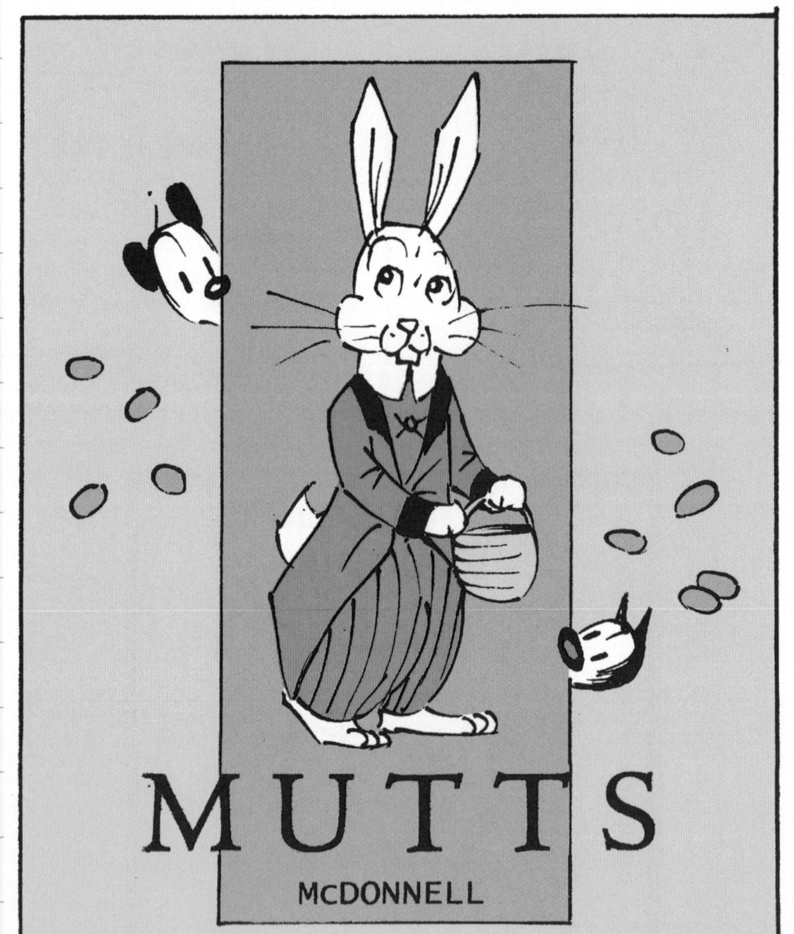
MUTTS
McDONNELL

ARE YOU THE EASTER BUNNY?
No.
SHUX.

I WAS HOPING FOR SHOME JELLY BEANS.

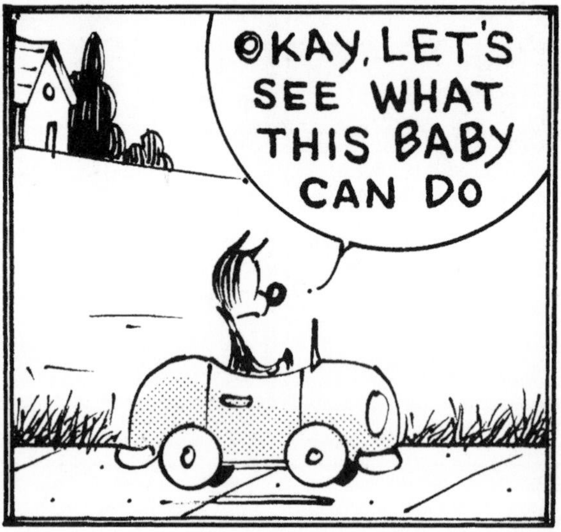
OKAY, LET'S SEE WHAT THIS BABY CAN DO

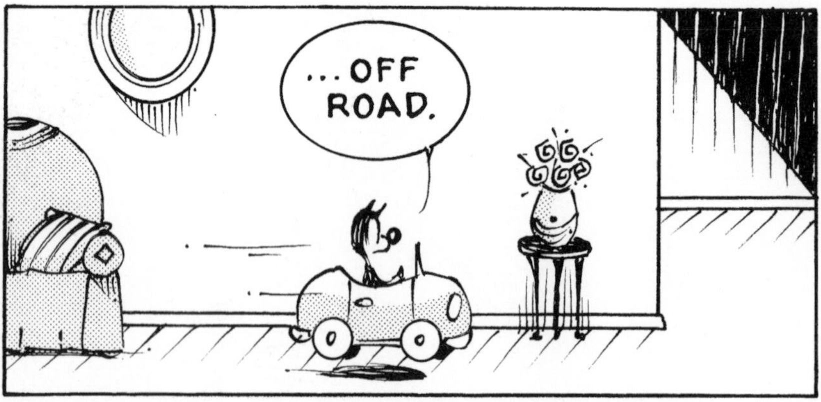
...OFF ROAD.

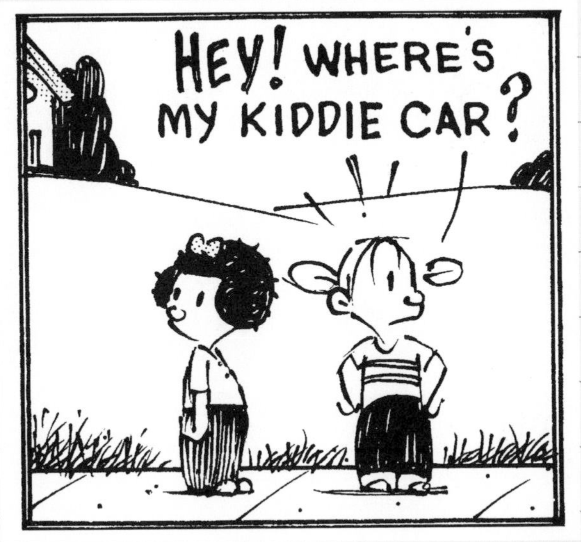
HEY! WHERE'S MY KIDDIE CAR?

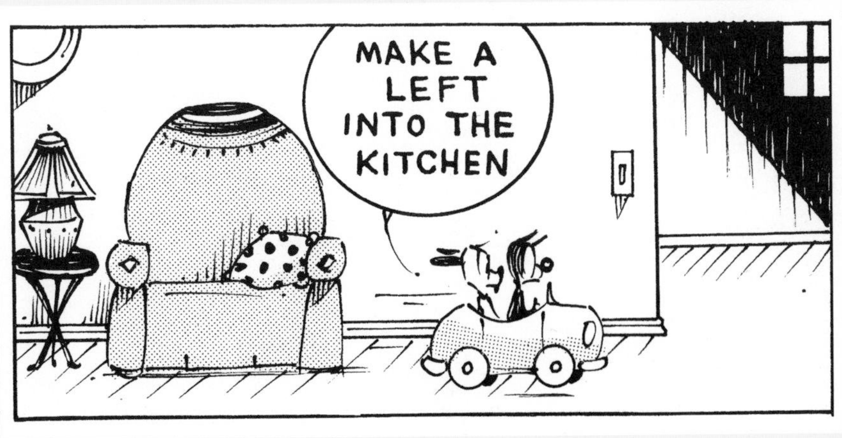
MAKE A LEFT INTO THE KITCHEN

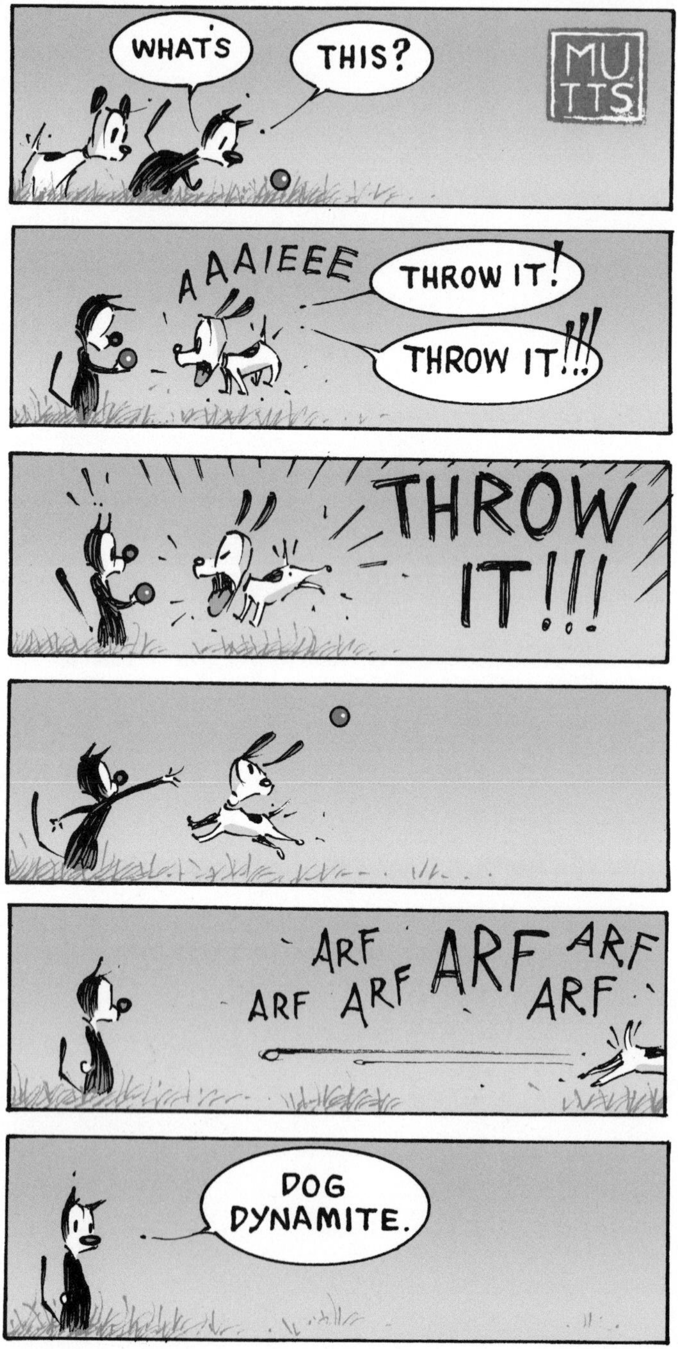
WHAT'S
THIS?
MUTTS
AAAIEEE
THROW IT!
THROW IT!!!
THROW IT!!!
ARF
ARF ARF
ARF
ARF
ARF
DOG DYNAMITE.

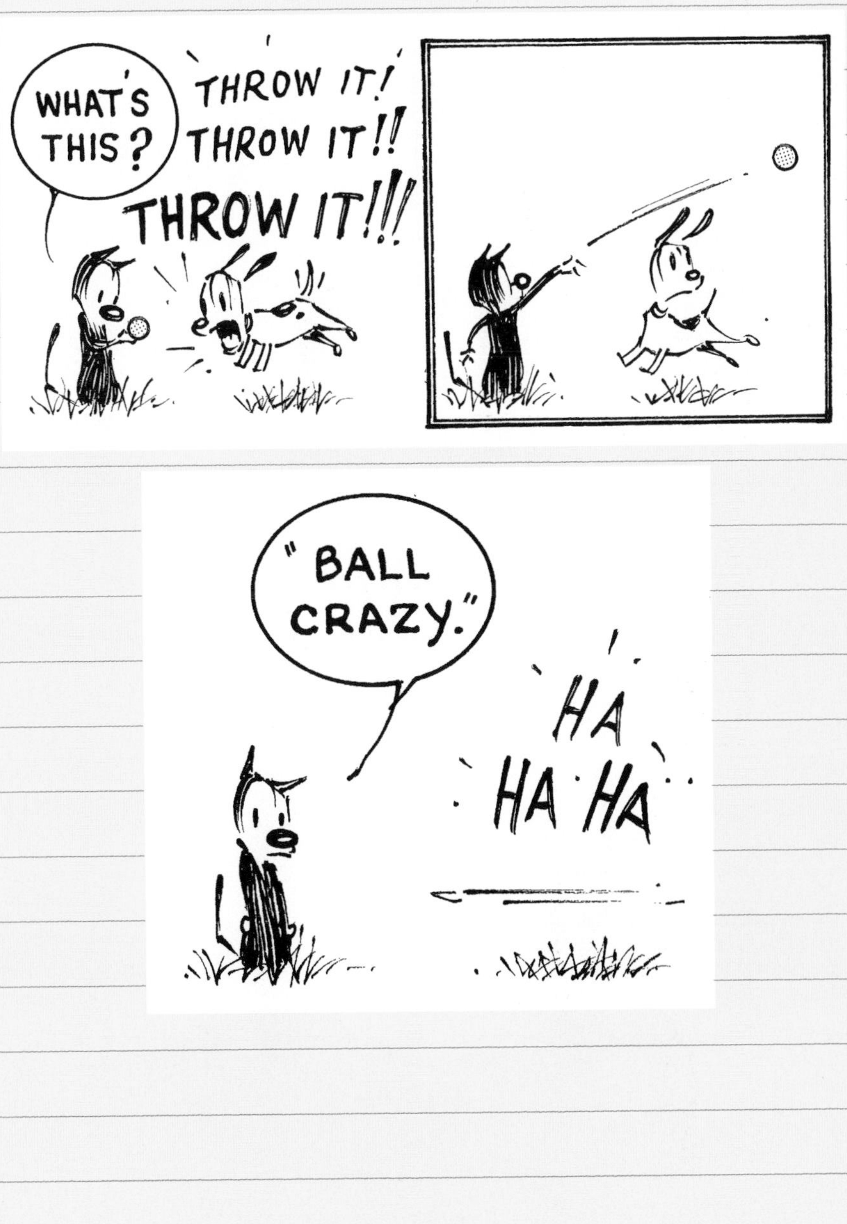
WHAT'S THIS?
THROW IT! THROW IT!! THROW IT!!!
"BALL CRAZY."
HA HA HA

THROW IT! THROW IT!
THROW IT! THROW IT!
THROW IT!!!
FETCH
WHERE CAN I HIDE?

EARL, YOUR MIND IS OBSHESSED WITH THIS BALL.— YOU **MUST** LET IT GO!
LET IT GO.
LET
IT
GO.

MOOCH, I APOLOGIZE FOR BEING SO "BALL CRAZY" BUT I THINK I GOT IT OUT OF MY SYSTEM.
WHAT'S THIS?
THROW IT! THROW IT! THROW IT! THROW IT! THROW IT!!!

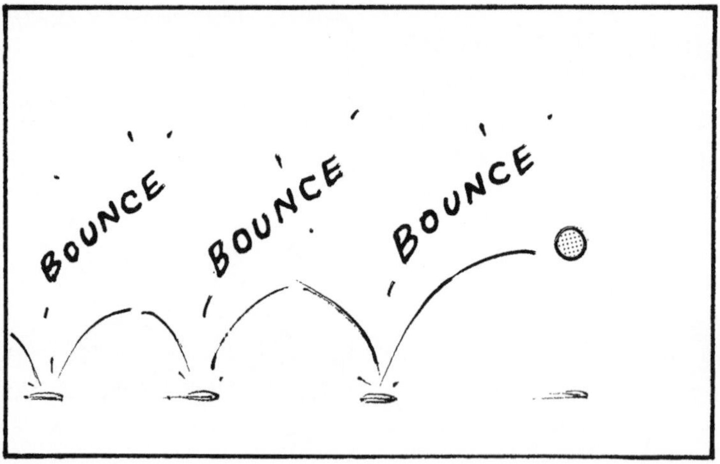
BOUNCE
BOUNCE
BOUNCE

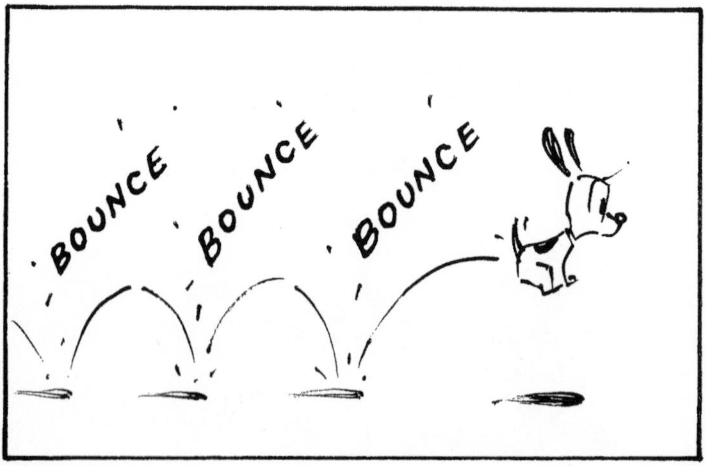
BOUNCE
BOUNCE
BOUNCE

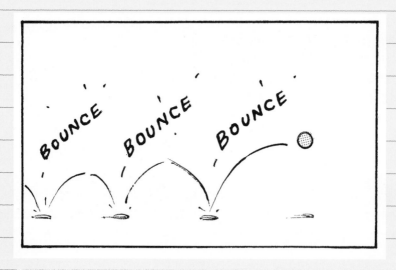

EARL, TAKE A LOOK AT THIS FUNNY-LOOKING ROCK
!!!
OH.

I'VE NEVER HAD A ROCK LOOK BACK!

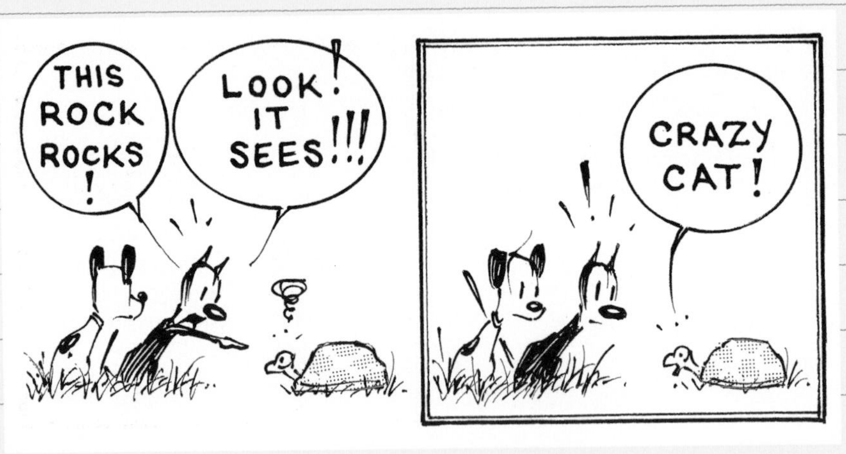
THIS ROCK ROCKS!
LOOK! IT SEES!!!
CRAZY CAT!

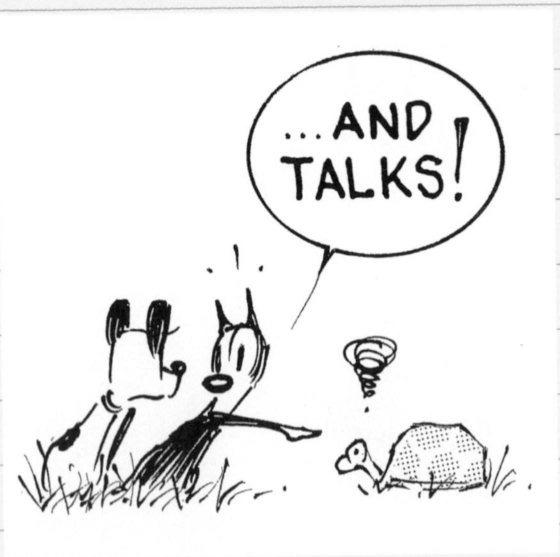
...AND TALKS!

I AM NOT A ROCK–I'M A TURTLE!
KISS
I LOVES TURTLES

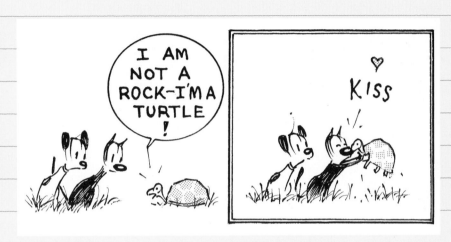

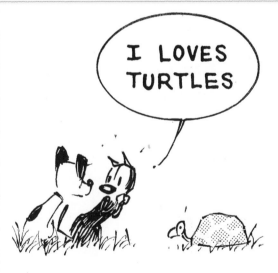

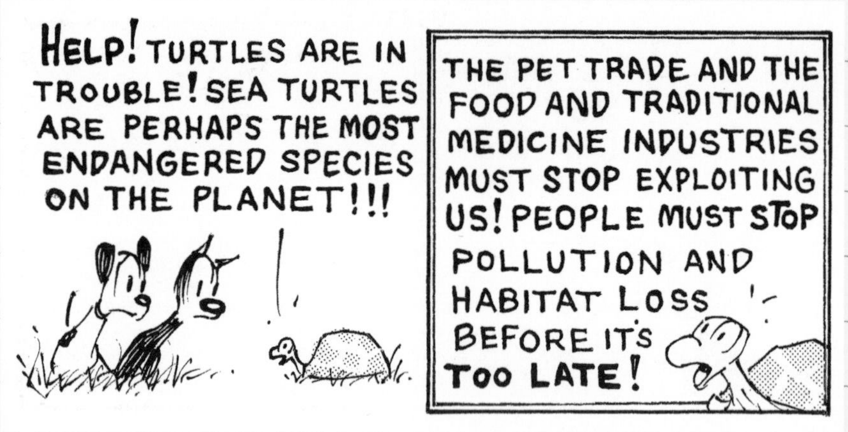
HELP! TURTLES ARE IN TROUBLE! SEA TURTLES ARE PERHAPS THE MOST ENDANGERED SPECIES ON THE PLANET!!!
THE PET TRADE AND THE FOOD AND TRADITIONAL MEDICINE INDUSTRIES MUST STOP EXPLOITING US! PEOPLE MUST STOP POLLUTION AND HABITAT LOSS BEFORE IT'S TOO LATE!

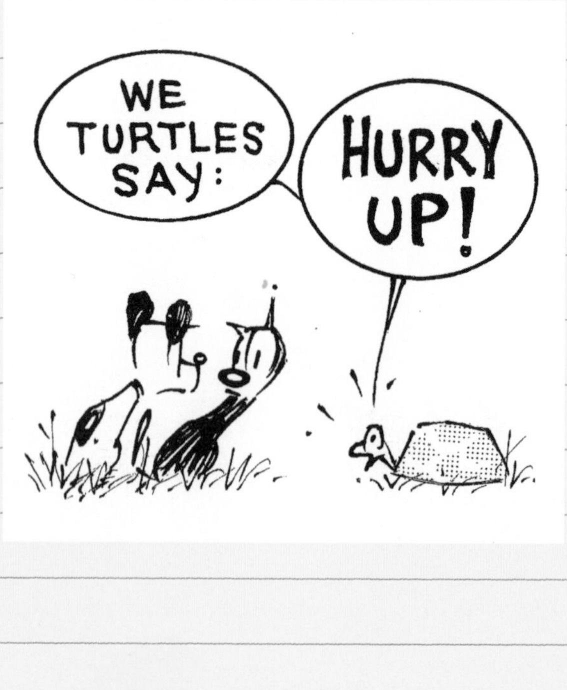
WE TURTLES SAY:
HURRY UP!

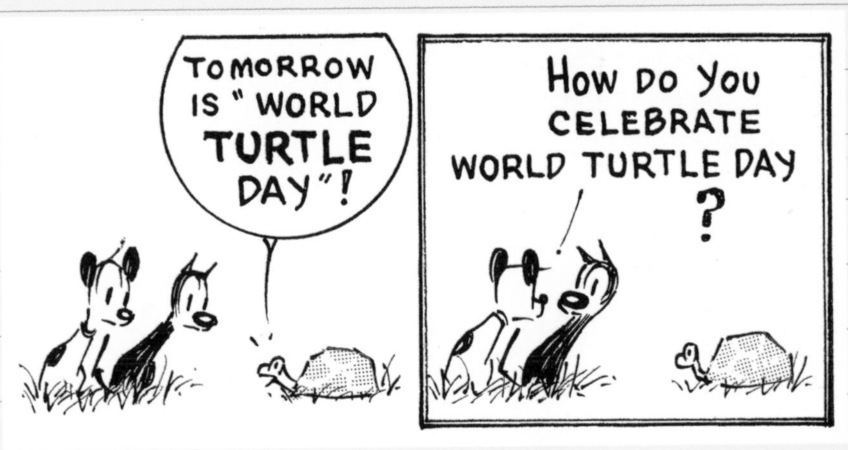
TOMORROW IS "WORLD TURTLE DAY"!
HOW DO YOU CELEBRATE WORLD TURTLE DAY ?

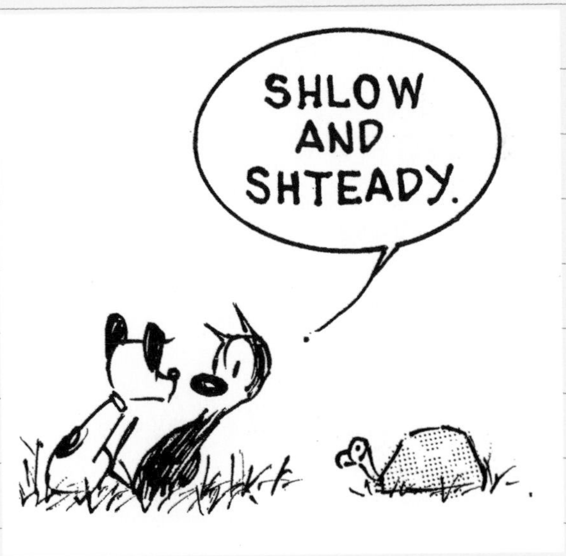
SHLOW AND SHTEADY.

HUG TIME!
!?!
HAPPY WORLD TURTLE DAY.

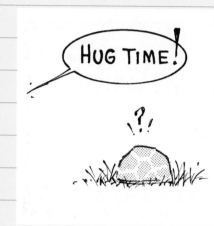

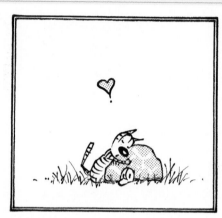

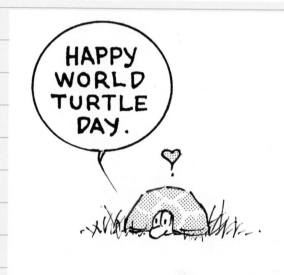

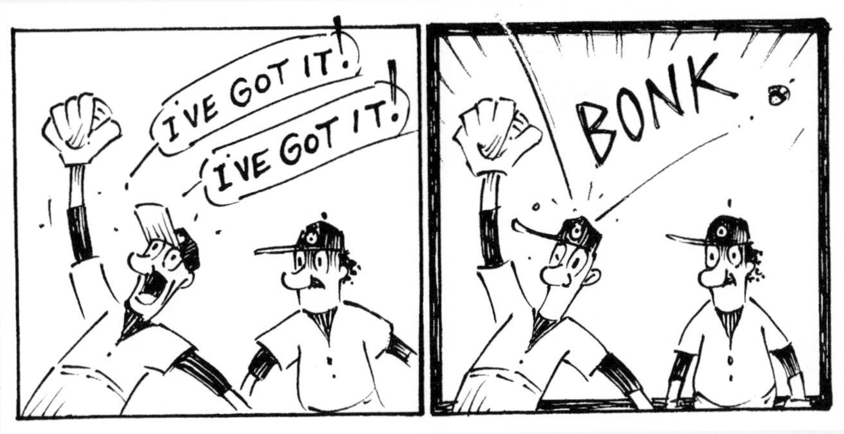
I'VE GOT IT!
I'VE GOT IT!
BONK

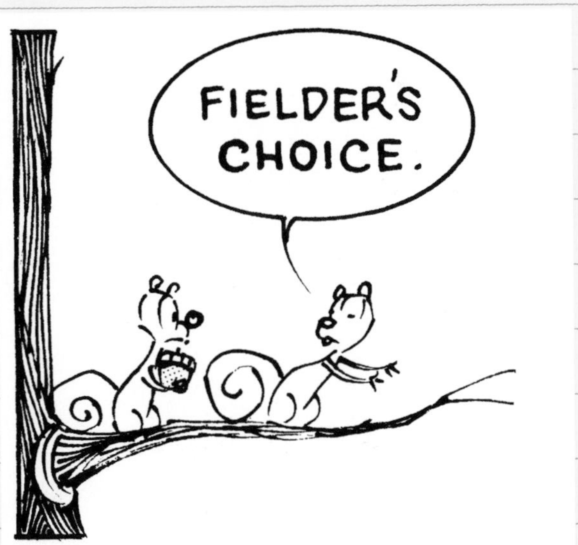
FIELDER'S CHOICE.

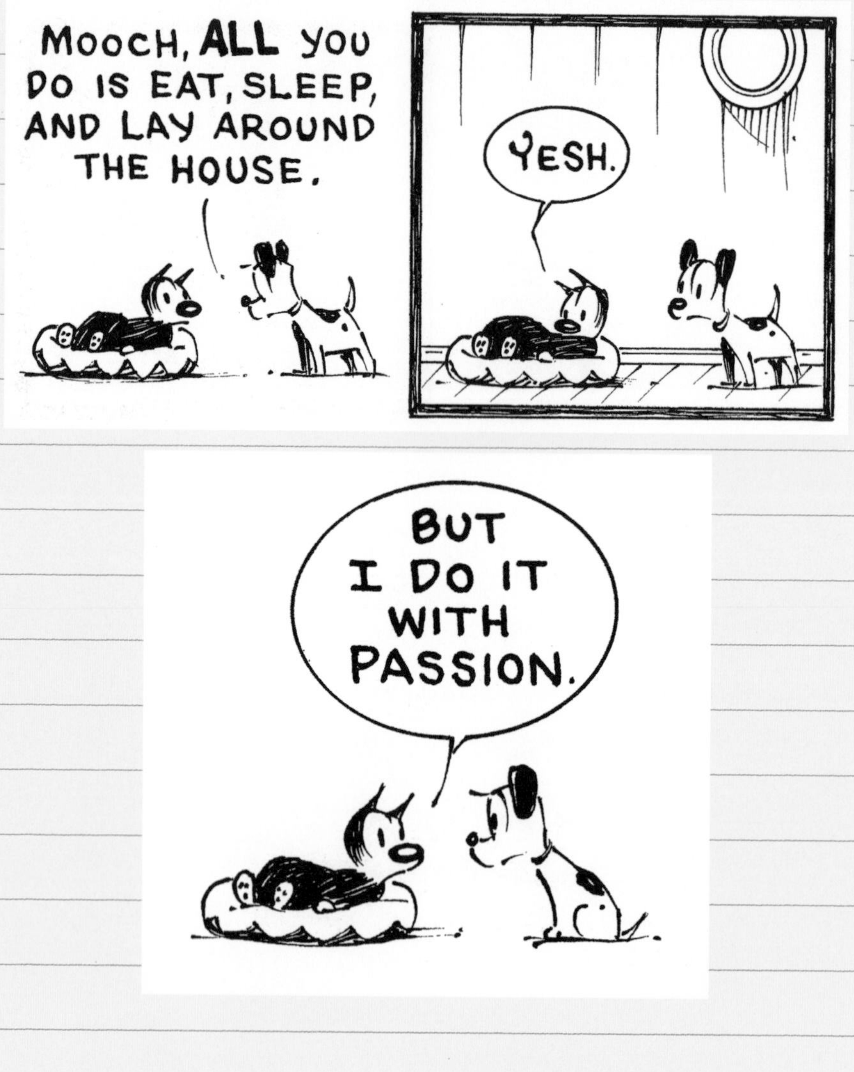
MOOCH, ALL YOU DO IS EAT, SLEEP, AND LAY AROUND THE HOUSE.
YESH.
BUT I DO IT WITH PASSION.

CHOMP
CHOMP CHOMP
Lick KISS
Lick Lick
KISS
MY COMPLIMENTS TO THE CHEF.

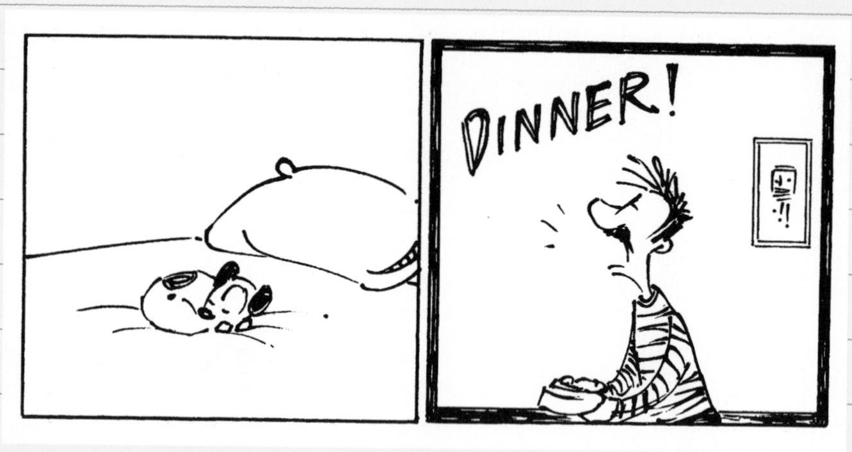
DINNER!

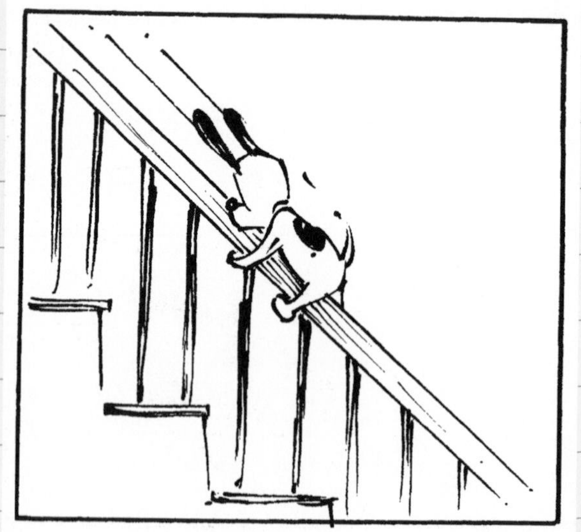

SHELTER STORIES
"LENNY"
PICK ME.
I KNOW A LOT OF TRICKS.

PICK A CARD— ANY CARD.

SHELTER STORIES
"LENNY"
PICK ME.
I GET ALONG WELL WITH CATS.

AFTER YOUR ICE CREAM I'LL BRUSH YOU!

SHELTER STORIES
"LENNY"
PICK ME.
I'D MAKE A GREAT GUARD DOG.

NOW TAKE OFF YOUR SHOES.
SECURITY

SHELTER STORIES
"LENNY"
PICK ME.
I'M EAGER TO PLEASE

LOOK
I CAN RIVER-DANCE

SHELTER STORIES
"LENNY"
PICK ME.
I'M VERY GOOD WITH CHILDREN.

"GOOD NIGHT ROOM, GOOD NIGHT MOON"

SHELTER STORIES
"LENNY"
PICK ME.
PLEASE

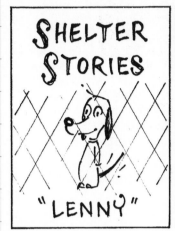

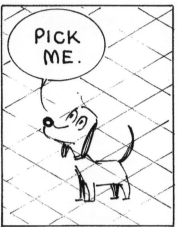

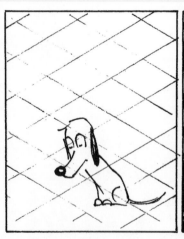

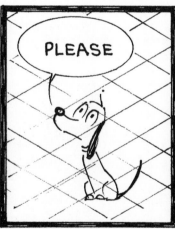

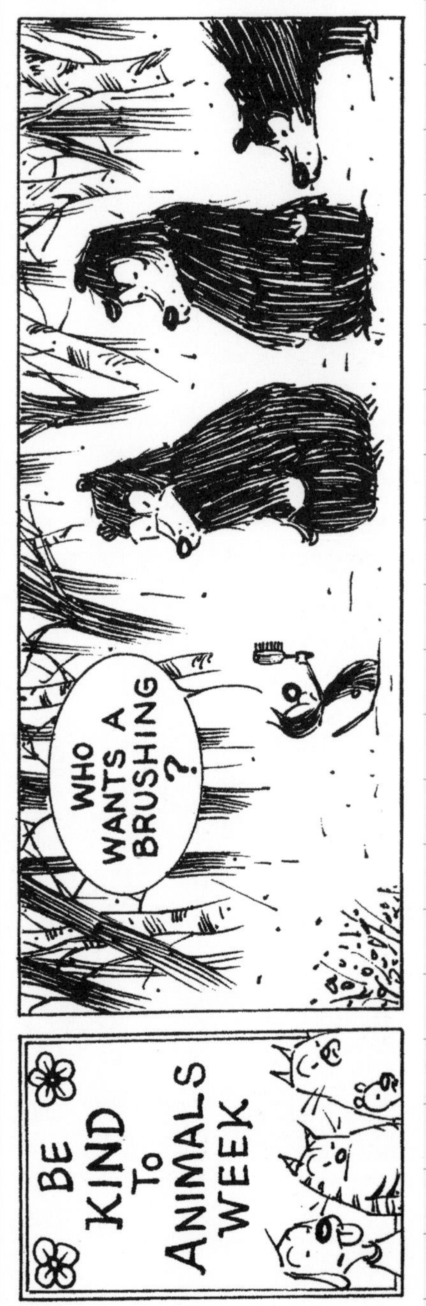
BE KIND To ANIMALS WEEK
WHO WANTS A BRUSHING?

GA-
GA-
GAK!
SOMEBODY LOVES THE NEW BIRDFEEDER.
OOOOH

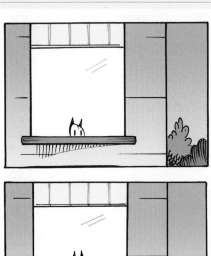

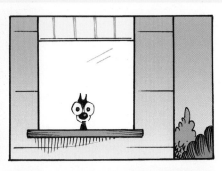

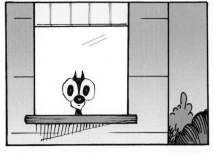

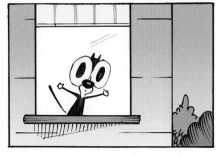

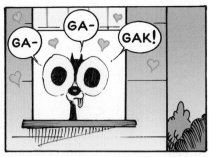

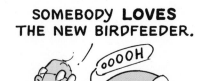

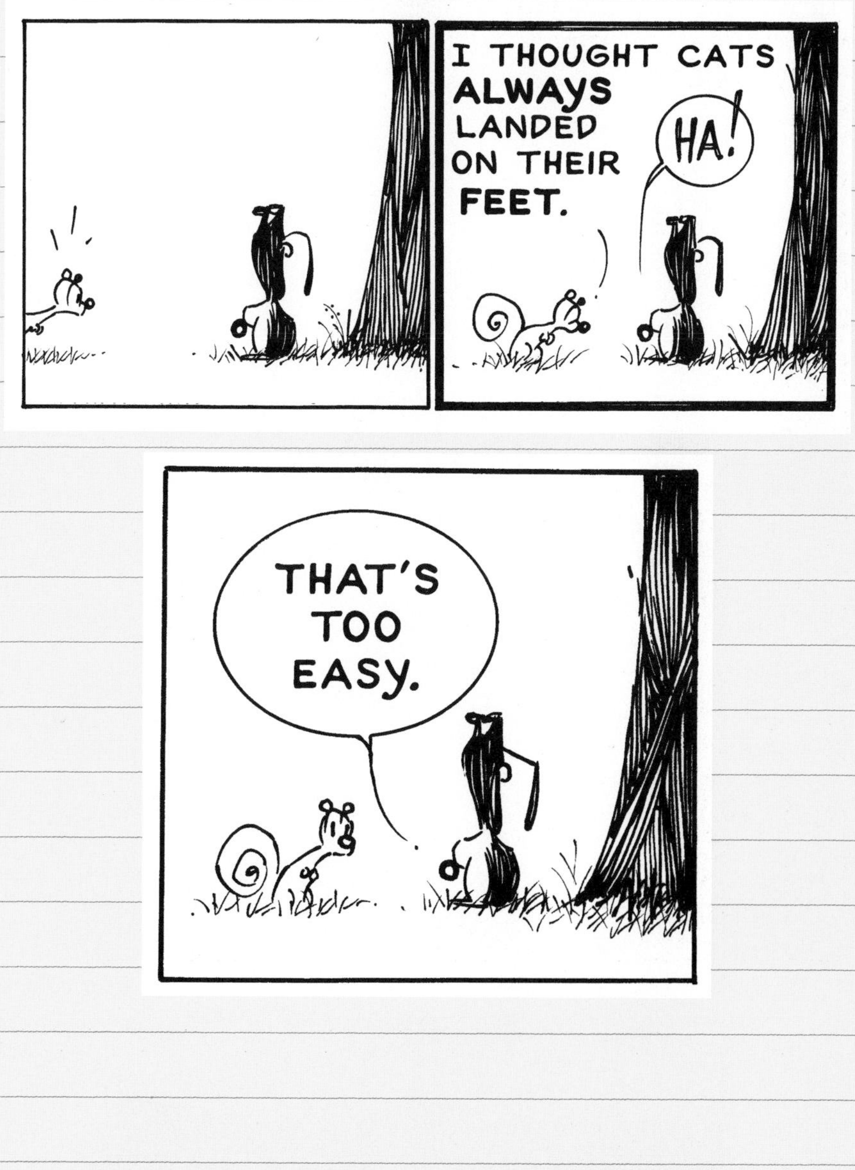
I THOUGHT CATS ALWAYS LANDED ON THEIR FEET.
HA!
THAT'S TOO EASY.

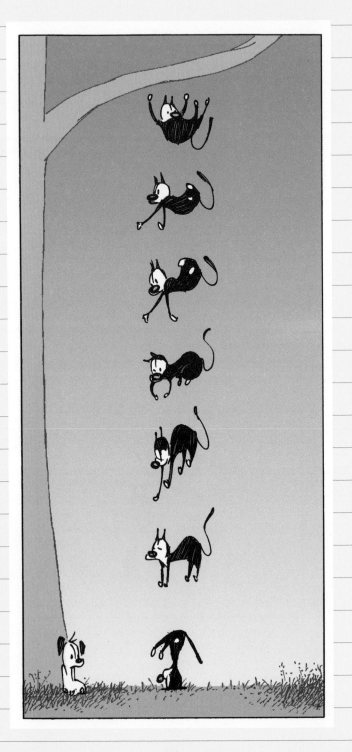

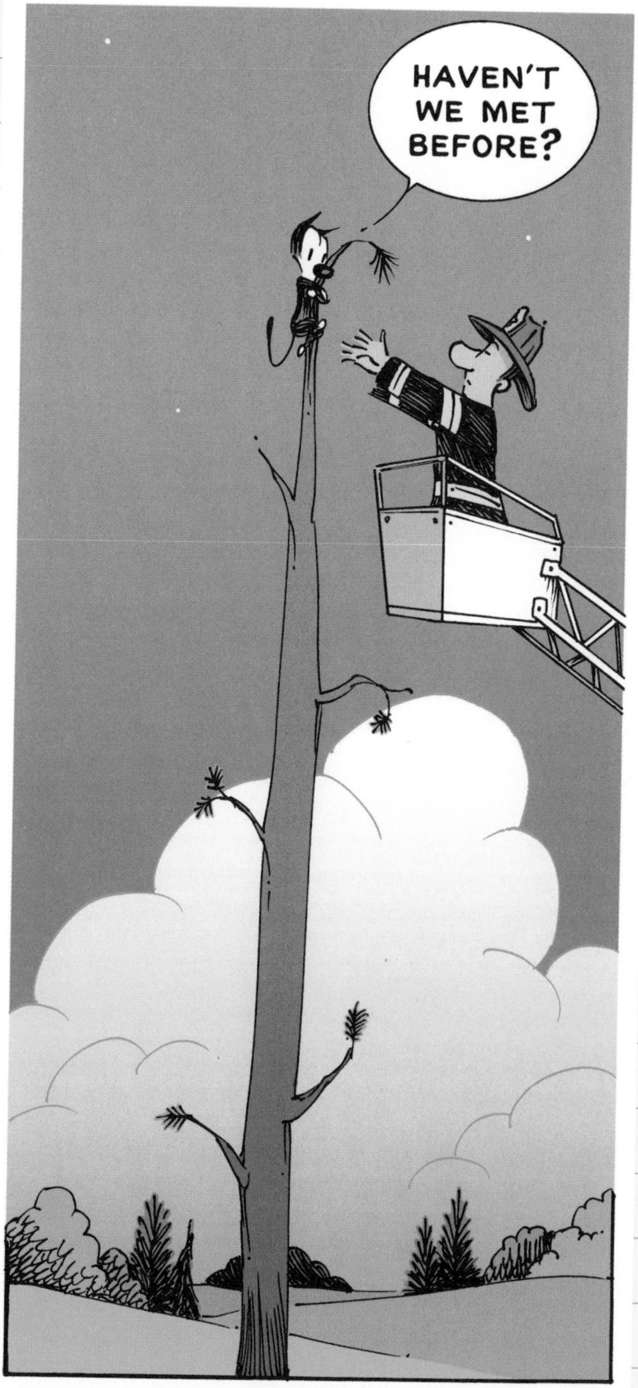
HAVEN'T WE MET BEFORE?

Mutts
by P. L. McDonnell

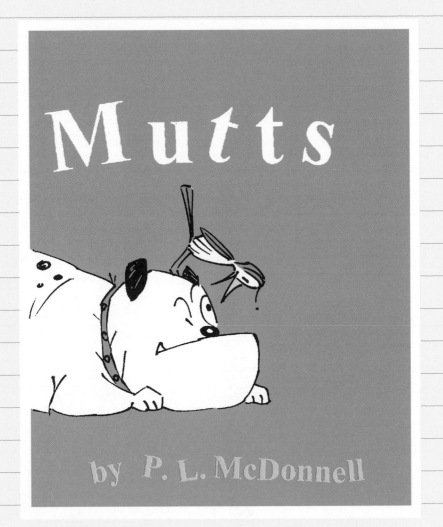

WHO ELSE WOULD GENTLY WASH YOUR DIRTY WITTLE FACE?
WHO ELSE WOULD KEEP YOUR WITTLE FOOTSIES WARM ALL NIGHT?
WHO ELSE WOULD REGURGITATE A BUGGY SNACK INTO YOUR HUNGRY WITTLE MOUTH?
WHO ELSE WOULD UNCONDITIONALLY LOVE AND PROTECT YOUR WITTLE SELF?
SIGH...
MOM

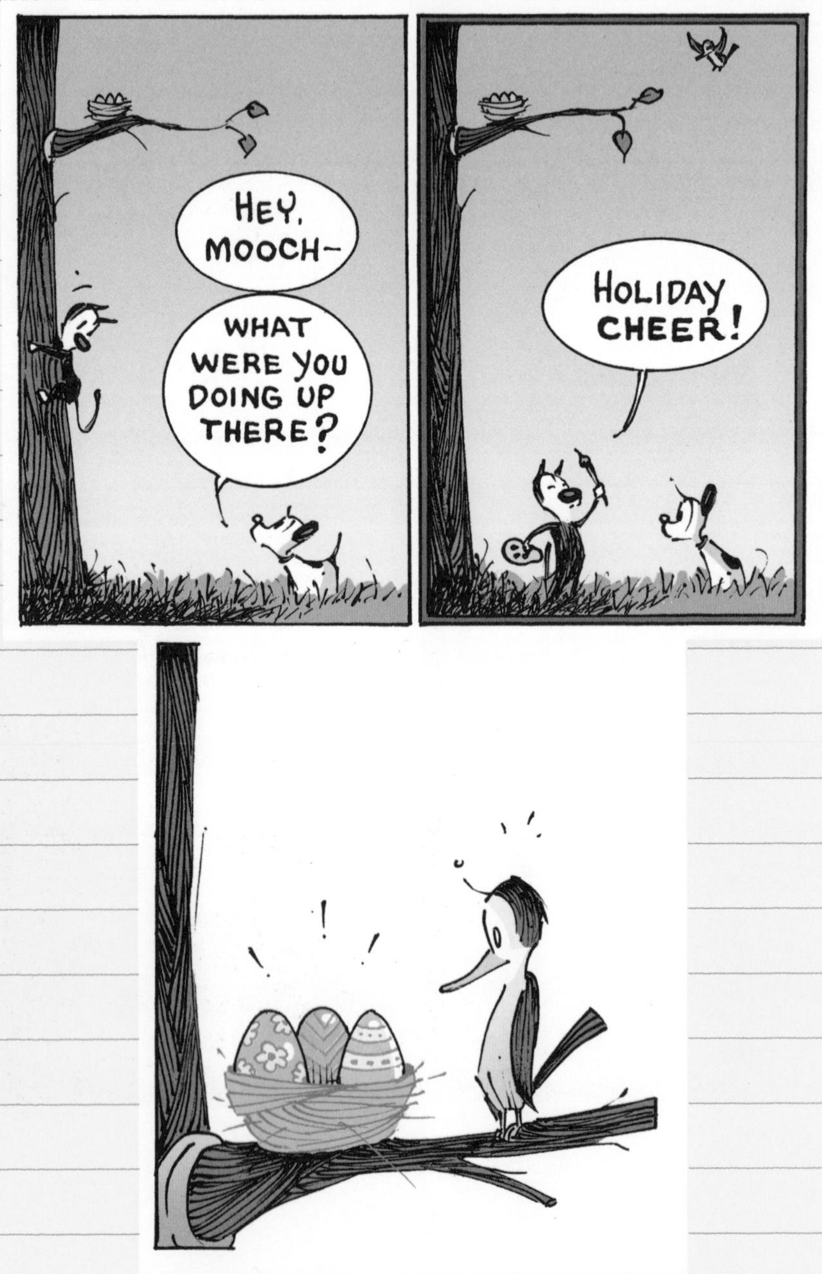
HEY, MOOCH-
WHAT WERE YOU DOING UP THERE?
HOLIDAY CHEER!

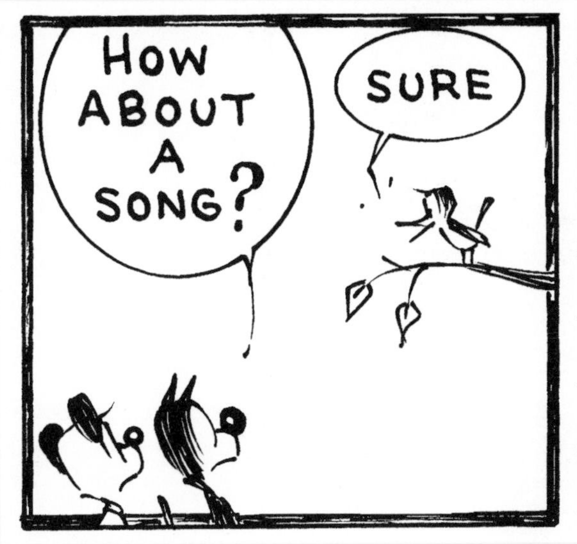
HOW ABOUT A SONG?
SURE

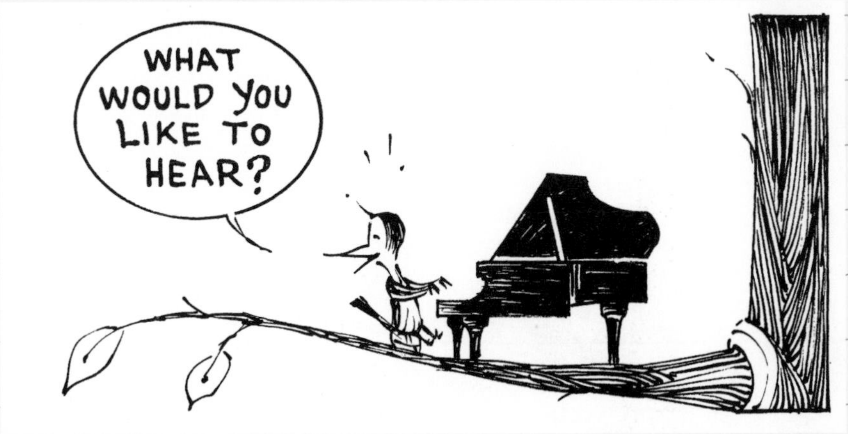
WHAT WOULD YOU LIKE TO HEAR?

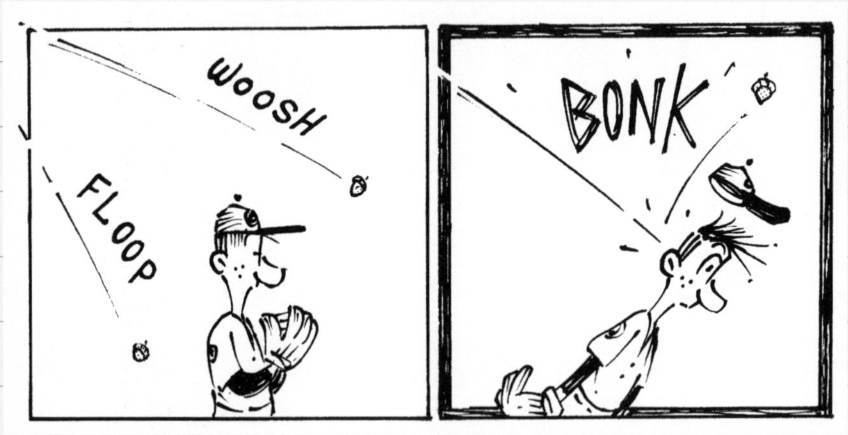
WOOSH
FLOOP
BONK

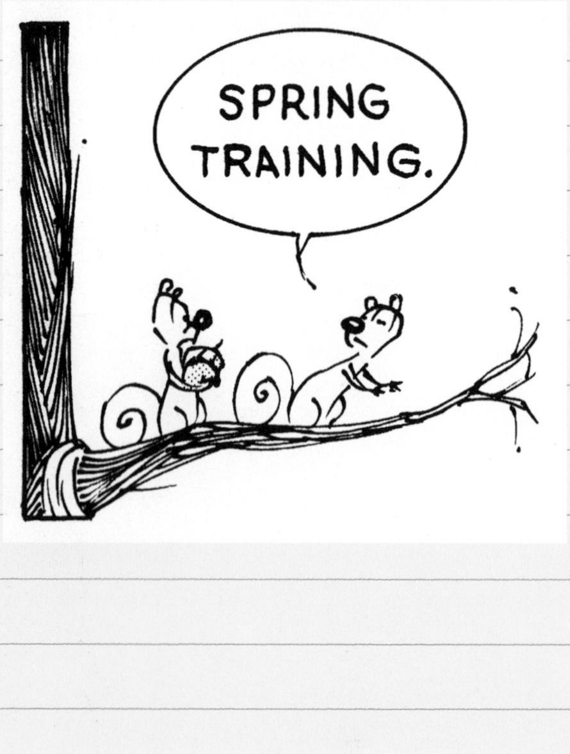
SPRING TRAINING.

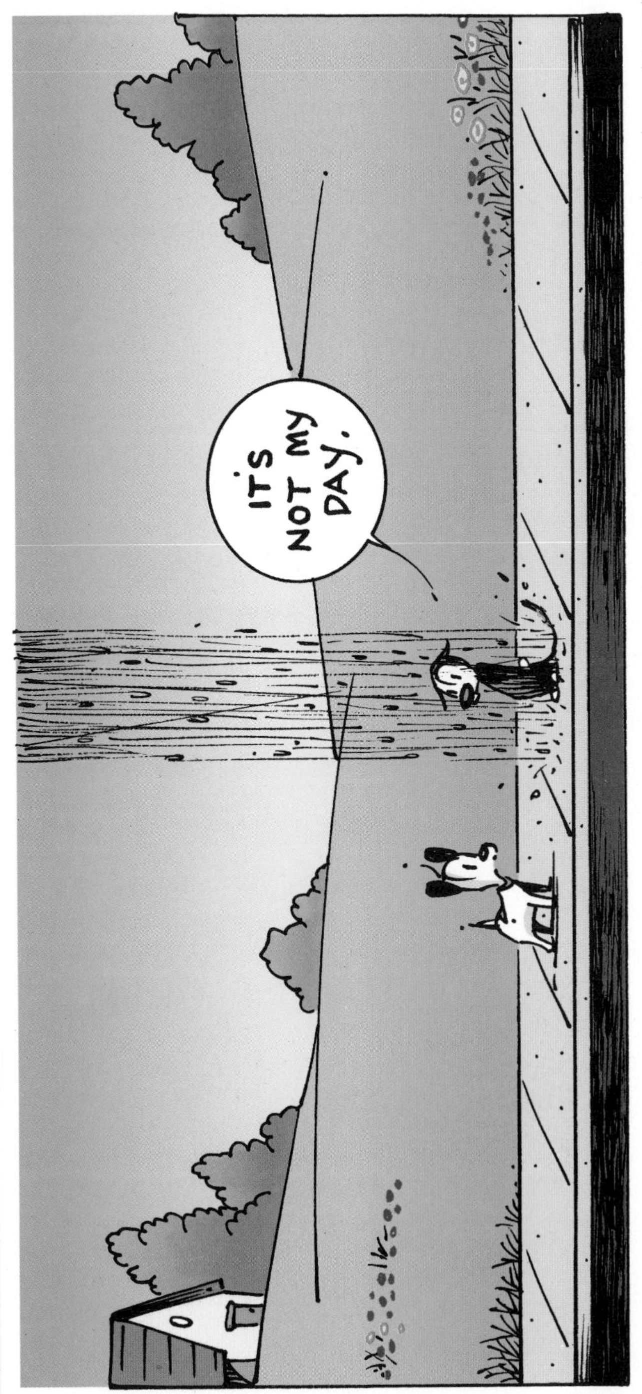
IT'S NOT MY DAY.

WHAT'S IT LIKE OUT, MOOCH?
ROTTEN —IT'S RAIN-ING.
I'LL TELL YA...
WE'RE LUCKY TO BE INSIDE WHERE IT'S NICE AND DRY.

MOOCH, YOU HAVE THAT "WILD" LOOK IN YOUR EYES AGAIN.
I DO?

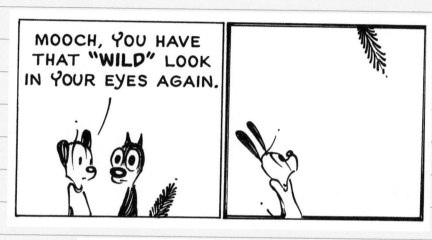

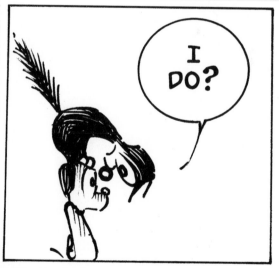

THE BIRDS ARE BACK
HMMM...
THAT GUY LOOKS FAMILIAR

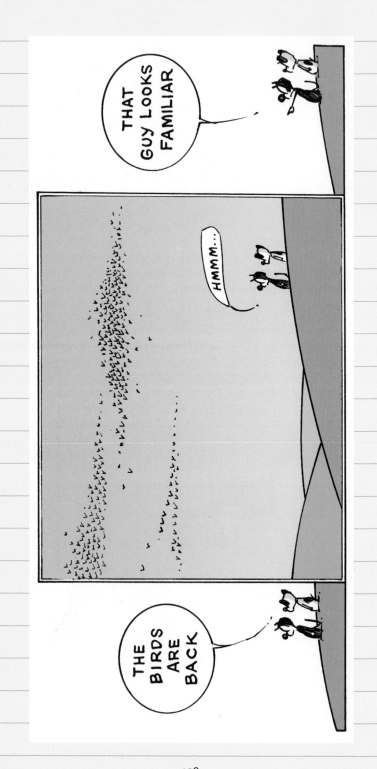

Z Z Z Z z
HEY! IT'S SHPRING! TIME TO WAKE UP!
WHA...

GIVE ME ANOTHER TEN DAYS.

IT'S MARCH 23RD!!! YOU'VE HAD PLENTY OF SHLEEP, WUZZY!
HA!
THERE WAS A DAY IN JANUARY...
I WAS UP ALL NIGHT!

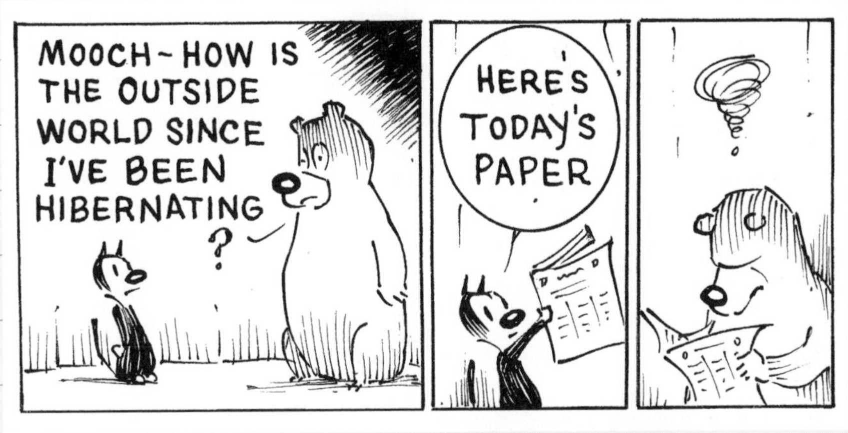
MOOCH - HOW IS THE OUTSIDE WORLD SINCE I'VE BEEN HIBERNATING?
HERE'S TODAY'S PAPER

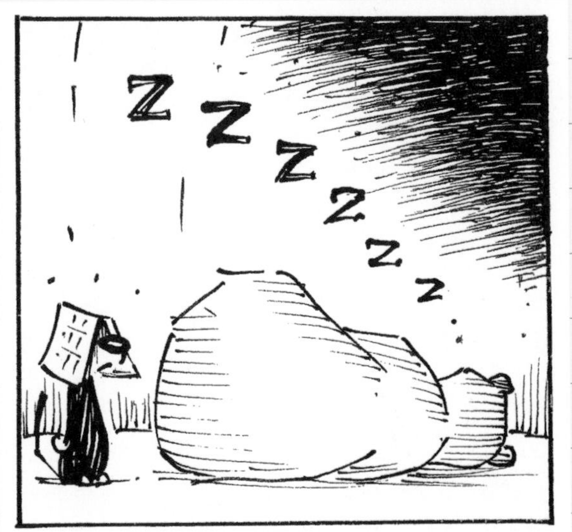
Z Z Z Z Z Z

GEE, MOOCH, I'VE BEEN ASLEEP FOR THREE MONTHS! I HAVE A **LOT** TO CATCH UP ON!
WHAT SHOULD I DO FIRST?

FIND YOUR TOOTH-BRUSH.

AHH... THREE MONTHS OF HIBERNATION FINALLY OVER!

I COULD USE A CUP OF COFFEE.

AHH, WHAT A BEAUTIFUL FEBRUARY DAY!
IT'S MARCH 27th!
I OVER-SLEPT.

SHELTER STORIES
"SCAMPI"
THERE'S A LOT OF CATS HERE AT THE SHELTER.
IT'S A REAL SWELL BUNCH OF GUYS AND GALS. SO—
COME ON DOWN—

I'LL HELP YOU CHOOSE ONE.

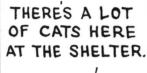

SHELTER STORIES
"SCAMPI"
THERE ARE MANY WONDERFUL TYPES OF CATS AT THE SHELTER
LONG HAIRS, SHORT HAIRS, CALICOS, TABBIES, SIAMESE
... GEE ...

I WOULDN'T KNOW **WHO** TO CHOOSE!!!

SHELTER STORIES
"SCAMPI"
YOU'RE ALL INVITED TO THE BIG "KITTY PARTY" AT THE SHELTER!
WHO KNOWS... YOU MIGHT GET LUCKY
... AND GO HOME WITH SOMEBODY.

SHELTER STORIES
"SCAMPI"
SO WE SAY COME TO THE SHELTER AND ADOPT THE PERFECT PET— A NICE KITTY!
ARF! ARF! ARF

DON'T LISTEN TO THEM.

SHELTER STORIES
"SCAMPI"
WHAT'S THAT!?!
YOU SAY YOU ARE GOING TO
ADOPT A CAT AT YOUR SHELTER—TODAY!!!

PURRR

SHELTER STORIES
"FIDO"
YOU'VE HEARD ALL WEEK ABOUT ADOPTING CATS
SO I JUST WANTED TO PUT IN A GOOD WORD FOR DOGS...
ARF.

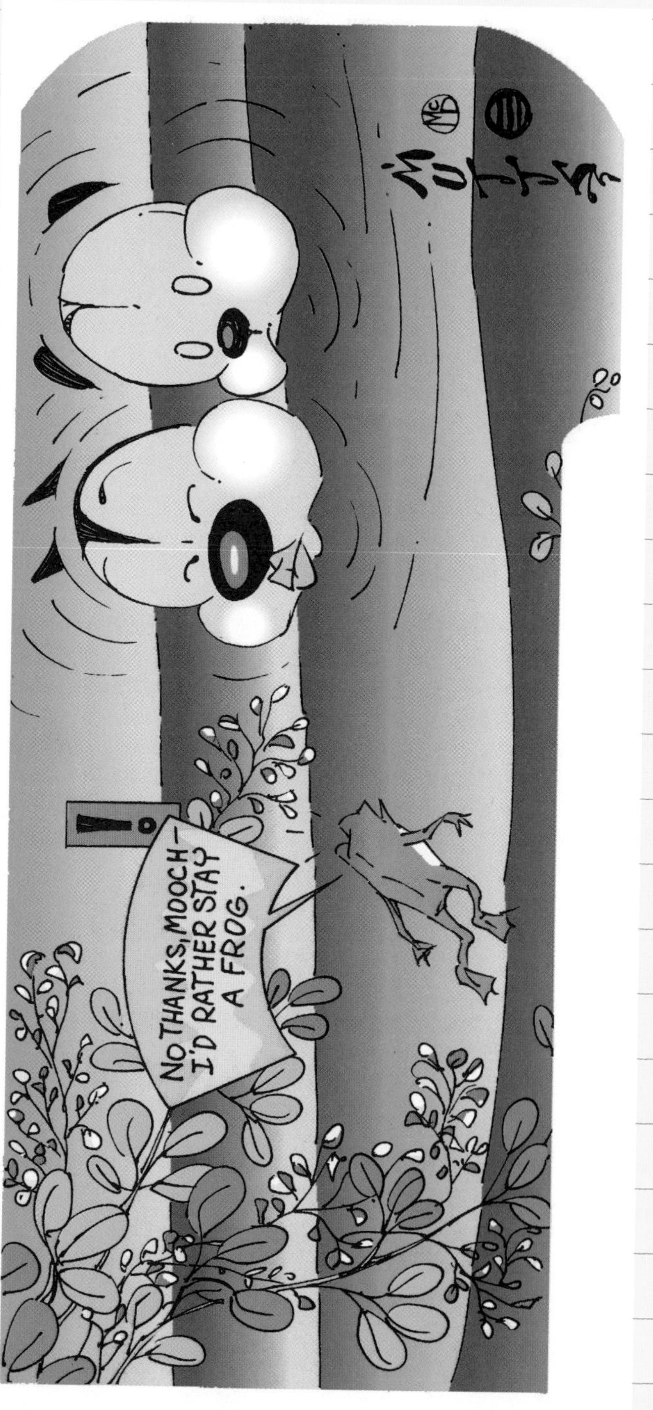
NO THANKS, MOOCH—
I'D RATHER STAY
A FROG.
!

MOOCH DREAMS of AFRICA
DO YOU HAVE A THROAT LOZENGE?

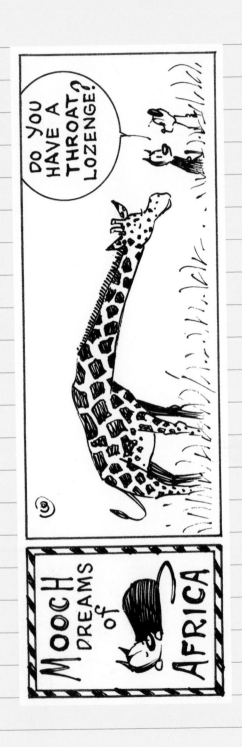

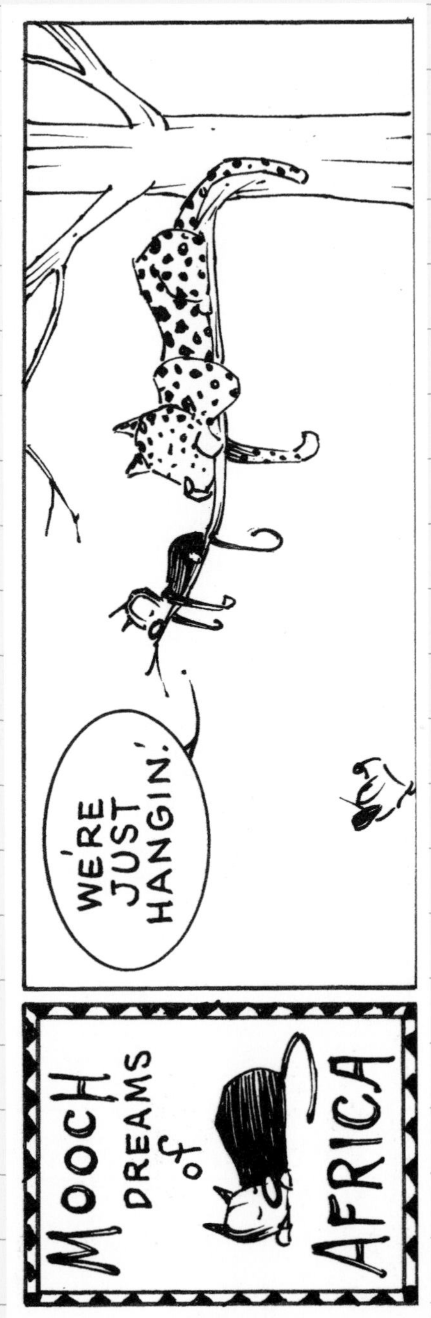
MOOCH DREAMS of AFRICA
WE'RE JUST HANGIN'!

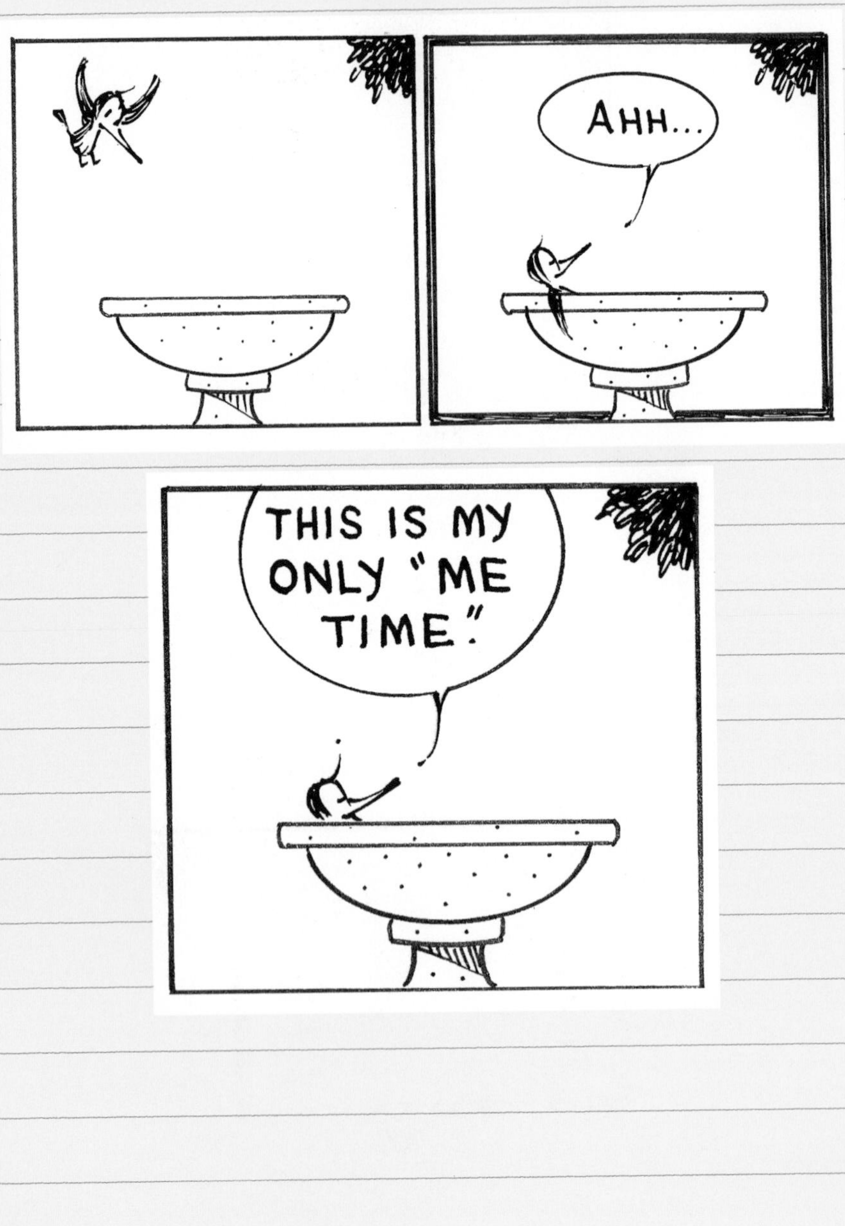
AHH...
THIS IS MY ONLY "ME TIME."

Spring is nature's way of saying,
"Let's party!"
~Robin Williams

DO
NOT
FEED
THE PIGEON.

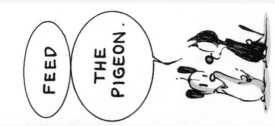

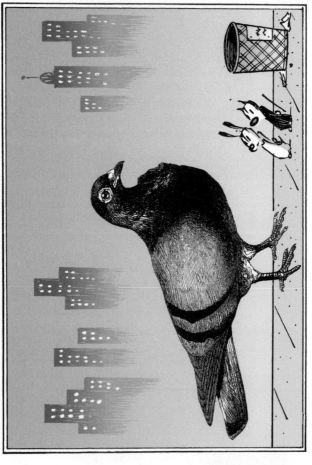

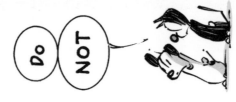

I SUPPOSE
I SHOULD TAKE THIS PERSON-ALLY.

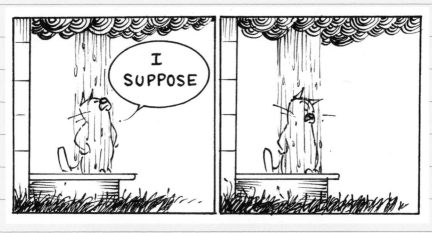

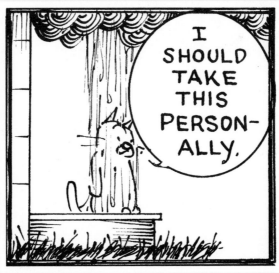

WHAT ABOUT THE FLOWERS !?!

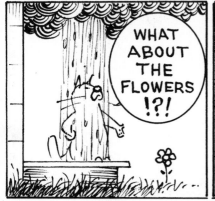

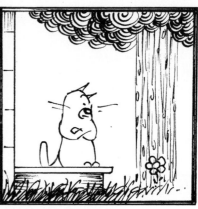

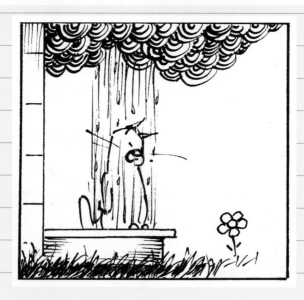

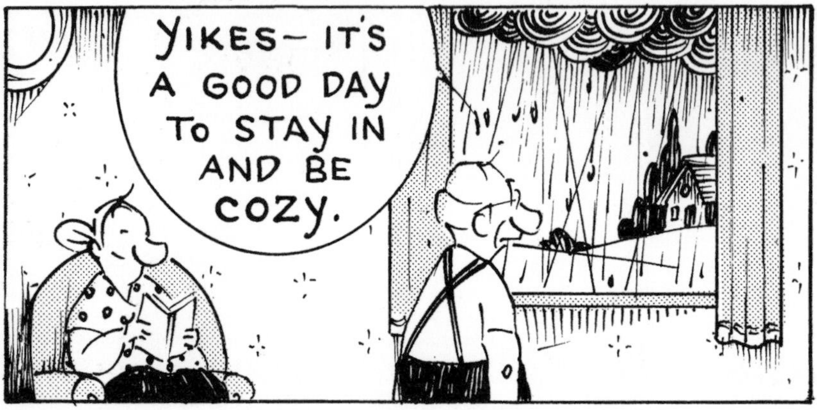
YIKES– IT'S A GOOD DAY TO STAY IN AND BE COZY.

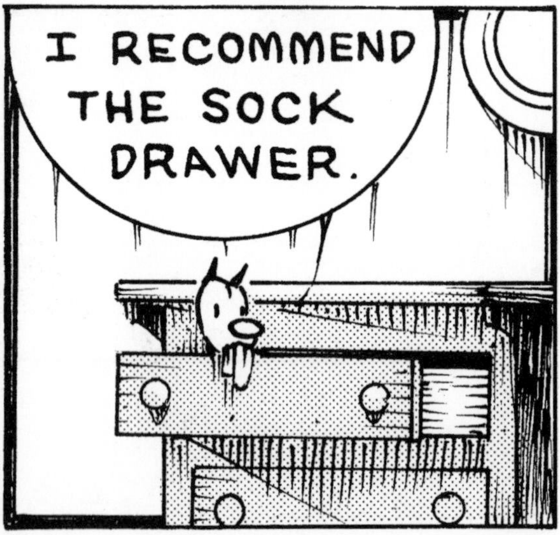
I RECOMMEND THE SOCK DRAWER.

WHEN'S EARTH DAY ?
SUNDAY.
GOOD

I PLAN TO BE THERE.

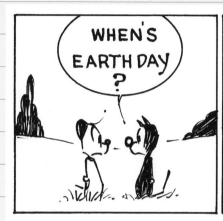

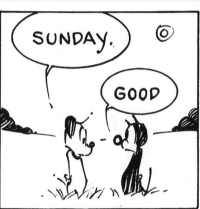

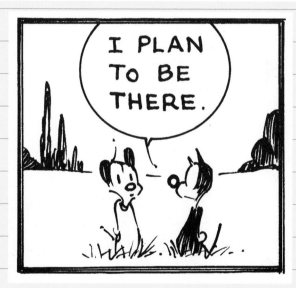

HEY, WORMY, GUESSH WHAT!
WHAT
SUNDAY'S EARTH DAY!
WOW
I CAN DIG THAT.

WE'VE TAKEN UP JOGGING.

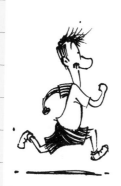

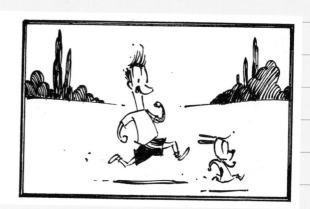

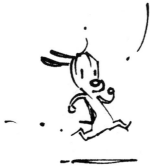

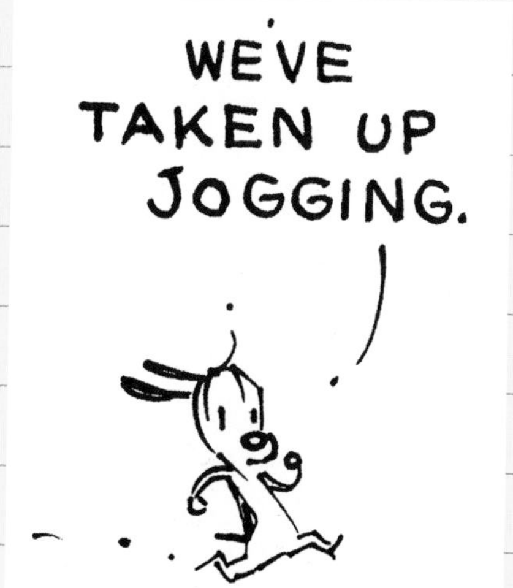

THINGS HAPPEN.

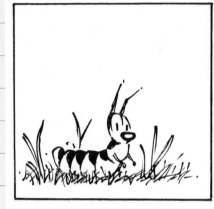

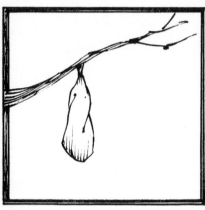

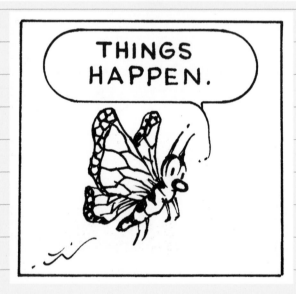

MOOCH-WHY ARE YOU WRAPPED UP IN A THROW RUG?
IT'S A **COCOON**! I'M GOING TO METASHMORPHOSE!
INTO WHAT!?!
WE'LL SEE.

EARL-I'M IN A RUG "COCOON" TO META-SHMORPHOSE INTO A BUTTERFLY.
SO...YOU'RE IN THE PUPA STAGE
WHA.?
No.

I HAVE A LITTER BOX FOR THAT.

WHAT MAKES YOU THINK YOU CAN METAMORPHOSE INTO A BUTTERFLY, MOOCH!?!
BUG LARVA DO IT!
SO!?!
SO...
CATS ARE SHMARTER

MOOCH-IT'S CRAZY! HOW ARE YOU GOING TO BECOME A BUTTERFLY!?!
HA! HOW DOES A CATERPILLAR DO IT?
I HAVE NO IDEA!
COULD YOU GO ASK?

WELL, MOOCH, YOU'VE BEEN IN YOUR "COCOON" FOR QUITE A WHILE NOW...
YESH
DO YOU THINK YOU ARE TURNING INTO A BUTTERFLY?
WELL...
I AM GOING A LITTLE BUGGY.

EARL– DID I METASHMORPHOSE? DO I HAVE WINGS?
NO– YOU'RE STILL JUST A **CAT**.

WELL, I GUESSH YOU CAN'T MESS WITH PERFECTION.

MORE TO EXPLORE! Featuring facts and activities about birds!

Peep's Bird Bistro

Mooch and Earl's friend Peep will appreciate this simple, easy-to-make bird feeder. Hang it from a tree outside your window and see which birds come to visit you!

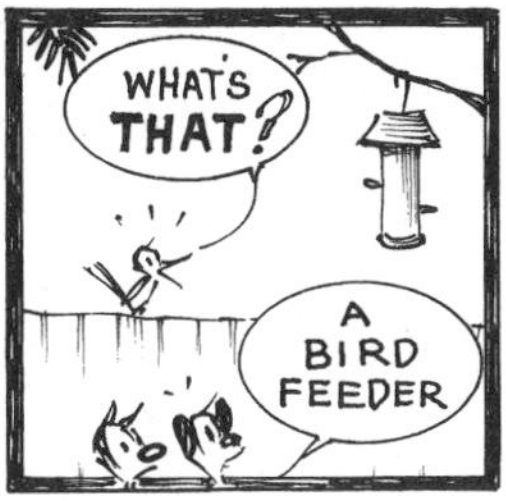
WHAT'S THAT?
A BIRD FEEDER

Supplies:

plastic bottle (remove all labels)
scissors
wooden spoon
birdseed
string

Instructions:

With the help of an adult, use the scissors to cut two holes on opposite sides of the bottle that are just wide enough for the spoon handle to fit through. The holes should be about 1.5 inches from the bottom of the bottle. The handle will go through one hole and out the other, making a perch for the bird.

Cut a small hole in the bottle about 1 inch above the perch. It should be about the size of a pea. If you're using larger seeds in your feeder (like sunflower seeds), you may need to cut a bigger hole. You don't want your feeder hole to be too big or else the seed will escape too quickly.

Slide the spoon through the perch holes, slowly fill your feeder, use the string to tie it to a tree branch, and voilà! You'll have a restaurant that's perfect for the frequent flyers in your neighborhood.

Eggs-traordinary Facts!

Have you ever stumbled upon a bird's nest and wondered about the egg that was resting inside it? Here are five fascinating facts about eggs and hatchlings that you might not have realized before:

- **Bird eggs** come in more colors than white and brown. They can be blue, green, beige, gray, red, orange . . . and even a combination of these colors.

- An **ostrich egg** can weigh up to five pounds, and it's about the size of a cantaloupe.

- **Hummingbirds** lay the smallest eggs of any bird. The eggs are about the size of a pea and weigh around ⅓ of a gram.

- The **incubation period** (the time it takes for an egg to hatch after it's been laid) varies from species to species. It can take anywhere from 10–11 days for smaller birds and up to 60–85 days for larger birds.

- The time it takes for a baby bird to fly after it hatches varies, too. **Western bluebirds**, for example, start to fly within 21 days, while cockatoo chicks begin trying to fly when they're around four months old.

Calls of the Wild

Many of us hear birds every day but don't think too much about what they might be saying. Birds call and sing for a number of reasons. Here are a few sounds you might hear on your next nature walk.

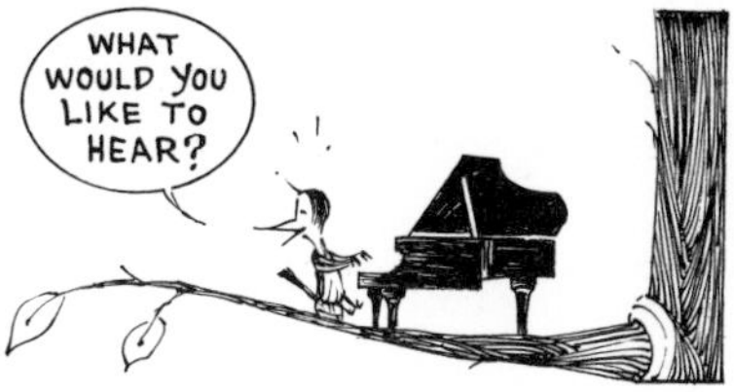
WHAT WOULD YOU LIKE TO HEAR?

Alarm calls

This call is often high-pitched, loud, and repeated over and over again. It's like a call to arms when a predator has been spotted, letting other birds know that danger is near.

Flight calls

When birds move through different territories—especially during migration—it's important for them to announce their presence to other birds while in flight. Flight calls are usually one or two notes, twitters, or buzzes that are softer and less piercing than alarm calls.

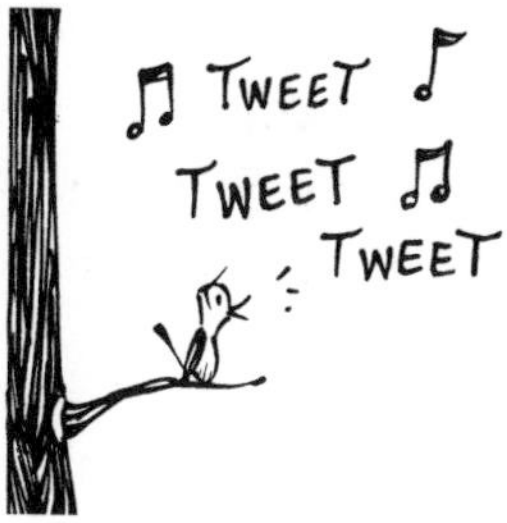
TWEET
TWEET
TWEET

Begging calls

Baby birds have their own kinds of calls (usually involving food). They cheep, peep, chirp, and even whine to get their parents' attention.

Courting songs

It's often the males that do the courting, and many species woo their mates through song. Songs are usually longer than calls and are made up of a series of notes with a clear pattern or melody.

Bird-Watching Scavenger Hunt

Earl and Mooch love to watch their feathered friends sing, soar, and sail through the breeze. You can, too! Here's a list of things to look for on your next bird-watching mission. Bring along a friend and see how many of these items you can check off your list.

Checklist

- ☐ A bird's nest
- ☐ A bird's feather
- ☐ A large bird*
- ☐ A small bird*
- ☐ A red bird*
- ☐ A blue bird*
- ☐ A black bird*
- ☐ Three or more birds together*
- ☐ A birdcall (1 or 2 notes)
- ☐ A bird's song (a series of notes together)

For an added challenge, see if you can find out the species of this bird by researching it online or in a reference book, and record your findings in a bird-watching journal. Keep notes on things like the bird's size, shape, distinctive features (like its feet, beak, or feather markings), actions, sounds, etc. to help you discover its identity.

Mutts is distributed internationally by King Features Syndicate, Inc. For information, write to King Features Syndicate, Inc., 300 West Fifty-Seventh Street, New York, New York 10019, or visit www.KingFeatures.com.

Andrews McMeel Publishing
a division of Andrews McMeel Universal
1130 Walnut Street, Kansas City, Missouri 64106

18 19 20 21 22 SDB 10 9 8 7 6 5 4 3 2 1

ISBN: 978-1-4494-8514-6

Library of Congress Control Number: 2016950283

Printed on recycled paper.

Mutts can be found on the Internet at www.mutts.com.

Cover design by Jeff Schulz

Made by:
Shenzhen Donnelley Printing Company Ltd.
Address and location of manufacturer:
No. 47, Wuhe Nan Road, Bantian Ind. Zone,
Shenzhen China, 518129
1st Printing — 10/23/17

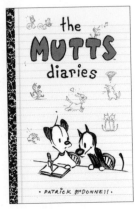

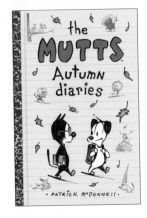

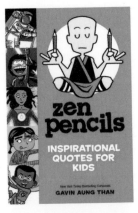
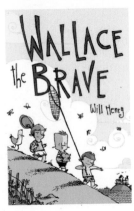